MONTANA RESCUE

SLEEPER SEAL SERIES BOOK #6

ELLE JAMES

TWISTED PAGE INC

MONTANA RESCUE

SLEEPER SEAL SERIES BOOK #6

Also part of the
Brotherhood Protectors Series

ELLE JAMES

New York Times & USA Today
Bestselling Author

EBOOK ISBN: 978-1-62695-088-7

ISBN PRINT: 978-1-62695-087-0

A NOTE TO THE READER

Thank you for purchasing a copy of MONTANA RESCUE! I hope you enjoy this, the 6th book in the Sleeper SEAL series of books. I'm super excited to be included with the delicious dozen writers who are penning tales in this world.

This whole idea of a group project started over a year ago at a conference. Several of us military romance authors thought it might be a fun idea to combine forces and talents to come up with a series that all of our readers might enjoy. Brainstorming ensued, and we had a concept involving former SEALs brought on to accomplish high-risk, secret projects.

I hope you enjoy seeing some of your favorite characters from the Brotherhood Protector Series. I love finding my way back to them in new stories. They remain a part of my life and thoughts, even though they are "only" fictional characters.

Elle James

AUTHOR'S NOTE

Enjoy other military books by Elle James

Brotherhood Protector Series
Montana SEAL (#1)
Bride Protector SEAL (#2)
Montana D-Force (#3)
Cowboy D-Force (#4)
Montana Ranger (#5)
Montana Dog Soldier (#6)
Montana SEAL Daddy (#7)
Montana Ranger's Wedding Vow (#8)
Montana Rescue
Take No Prisoners Series
SEAL's Honor (#1)
SEAL's Ultimate Challenge (#1.5)
SEAL'S Desire (#2)
SEAL's Embrace (#3)
SEAL's Obsession (#4)
SEAL's Proposal (#5)
SEAL's Seduction (#6)
SEAL'S Defiance (#7)
SEAL's Deception (#8)
SEAL's Deliverance (#9)

Visit ellejames.com for more titles and release dates

For hot cowboys, visit her alter ego Myla Jackson at
mylajackson.com
and join Elle James and Myla Jackson's Newsletter at
Newsletter

CHAPTER 1

Sleep was overrated. At least, that's what Caleb "Mad Dog" Maddox told himself as he paced the front porch of the mountain cabin, staring up at the stars in the sky. No street or porch lights marred the inky expanse, allowing the stars to twinkle unchallenged in the heavens over his little slice of hell in the Colorado Rockies.

Not that Colorado was hell. It didn't matter where Mad Dog landed. If it wasn't back with his Navy SEAL unit, fighting the good fight, it was hell.

He sat on the porch steps and rubbed at his sore knee, cursing the doctors who'd medically retired him from active duty before he could rain fire and destruction on the people who'd shot down his SEAL team's helicopter, ending his career and, more importantly, ending Frito's life.

Frito, Juan Federico Hernandez, had been one of the

newest SEALs on the team. The mission that ended it all was Frito's fifth and final.

Mad Dog couldn't complain too loudly about being kicked off the team when he was still alive and he didn't have a family depending on him. Frito had left behind a young wife and a baby girl. And he'd left behind memories of his incredible capabilities, loyalty and friendship in Mad Dog's mind. Most of all, he'd left behind the memory of his last minutes, before the life was crushed from his body.

They'd completed a secret mission in Syria, targeting a high-profile ISIS leader. Oh, they'd killed their target, decapitating the head of one of the ISIS snakes leading their followers to rape, pillage and burn —tactics they employed against the poor, defenseless people of Syria.

They'd made the hit and were on the helicopter during the extraction portion of the operation, when some bastard of an enemy fighter plugged them with an RPG. The round hit the tail of the helicopter, causing it to spiral toward the earth, flinging unsecured men out of the fuselage like so much confetti.

Mad Dog had twisted his hands into a nearby harness and held onto Frito, but the centrifugal force pulled the man out of his grip and flung him to the ground. Mad Dog lost his grip on the harness and slipped out as well, right before the helicopter landed. His fall was a mere seven or eight feet. Frito's had been from ten or twelve. The height of the fall didn't matter. The helicopter crashed down on top of Frito.

Whether he'd died in the fall or when the helicopter's wheel planted fully on his chest, the man was dead. Nothing Mad Dog could do would bring him back.

What if he'd held on just a few seconds longer? What if he'd let Frito climb into the helicopter first? What if he'd found his friend Ronin sooner and gotten him on board quicker? Would that have given Frito time to get in, get harnessed and stay alive?

Questions like these served no purpose, but he lived with them every time he closed his eyes at night. Not one of the what-if scenarios running through Mad Dog's mind changed the outcome.

Which led to more sleepless nights than he could count.

He'd come to Colorado after talking to his former teammate, Boomer. When Boomer had heard about Mad Dog's situation, he'd offered him the use of a friend's cabin in the Rocky Mountains.

The cabin's owner, Joseph "Kujo" Kuntz, had landed a job with the same folks Boomer worked for, a company headed by former Navy SEAL, Hank Patterson. Mad Dog remembered Hank. He'd worked with Hank when he'd first been assigned to SEAL Team 10.

Hank had left the Navy to help his father on his ranch in Montana and ended up establishing a personal security group of former Special Ops guys.

Mad Dog didn't dig too deeply into what kind of jobs Boomer and Kujo did or what their missions were. Frankly, he didn't care. Nothing mattered anymore. His life was irrelevant. Being a SEAL had been everything to him. He'd gone from a punk kid on the streets of

Houston to a respected member of an elite group of fighters. Now, he'd lost everything.

Who would have thought the punk-ass teen with a chip on his shoulder would have made something of his life? Granted, he might not have become a SEAL if he hadn't nearly killed a man.

One of his old friends died of an overdose on some dirty heroine. Mad Dog had chased down the drug dealer and beat the shit out of him, nearly killing the guy.

The drug dealer got off with a light sentence, some community service or some other bullshit like that. But the judge had looked Mad Dog square in the eye and told him he had two choices—go to jail for assault and battery or join the military where he could put his fighting skills to better use.

Mad Dog chose to join the Navy rather than go to jail. But he had his father partly to thank for giving him the drive to succeed. When the judge had his final say, Mad Dog's father snorted and said, "That kid won't ever amount to much."

Yeah, he hadn't gotten along with his father. All the man did for him was provide a roof over his head and the occasional food to fill his belly. No love had been lost between them.

Mad Dog's mother had left them when he was eight years old. She was probably tired of the verbal and physical abuse her husband heaped on her. Mad Dog didn't blame her for leaving, but he hated her for not taking him with her.

With hate in his heart, no family to go home to and a

desire to prove his father wrong, Mad Dog entered the military, worked his ass off and earned a spot in BUD/S training to become a SEAL.

It was during training that he'd learned some hard lessons about teamwork and looking out for your buddy. Out of pure cussedness, he'd suffered through the worst of the worst to become one of the best of the best.

Unfortunately, his father died halfway through Mad Dog's BUD/S training. He'd never had the satisfaction of showing his father how wrong he was.

The man had died how Mad Dog always imagined he would—when his trailer caught fire. His father had been asleep in his ratty recliner with beer cans strewn across the floor. The police report stated they suspected alcohol was involved. No kidding. Frank Maddox was a horrible drunk.

He hadn't felt much of anything upon the news of his father's death. The cadre at BUD/S offered to let him go home for the funeral. Mad Dog said hell no. He had no love for the man whose only gift to him had been the gift of life. And he sure as hell wasn't going to start the BUD/S training all over from scratch. No fucking way. He'd made it through Hell Week by then. No sane person went through Hell Week twice, if he could help it.

Upon graduation from BUD/S, he'd been assigned to a SEAL team. Not only had he proven his father wrong, he'd finally found people he could call his family. Through some pretty hairy missions, he'd bonded with his teammates.

He'd do anything for them, and they always had his back. They were the brothers he never had growing up, the family he'd always longed for.

Now he had none.

Sometimes, he wished he had been the one crushed beneath the helicopter instead of Frito.

The sun edged up over the horizon, spilling liquid gold across the mountains and warming the chill in the air. The beauty was not lost on Mad Dog. He'd always wanted to live in the mountains, away from the noise and smells of Houston, the traffic, hordes of people and the oil refineries. But he hadn't pictured being alone in the mountains.

After joining SEAL Team 10, he'd started thinking about having a real family, like what Frito had. A good woman to share his life with, to be there when he came home. Why not? His buddies on the team had succumbed to love. Mad Dog had begun to believe it could happen to him.

Until his career ended with one rocket-propelled grenade hitting the helicopter he flew inside.

Mad Dog pushed to his feet and walked barefoot across the moss-covered ground to a rocky ledge not far from the cabin. He'd spent many days and nights standing there, contemplating what was left of his life. Today, he contemplated how long it would take for him to fall from the top of the cliff to the bottom two-hundred and fifty feet below.

He was tired. Tired of the boredom, tired of the guilt and tired of being alone. Every day was just like the last. With no purpose in his life, what was the use of living?

No one relied on him to help out in a tight situation. His team continued on, without him. They didn't need a SEAL with a bum leg. Once a SEAL, always a SEAL... Ha!

He stared down at the jagged boulders. Ending it here would prove what? That his father was right after all? That he'd never amount to much? That all the sweat, pain and hard work he'd put into becoming a SEAL hadn't accomplished a fucking thing?

Mad Dog took one step, then another, toward the cliff's edge.

A honk sounded nearby, disturbing the utter silence, the sound incongruous with the mountainous surroundings.

Another honk, closer still, echoed off the hillsides.

Irritated by the interruption, Mad Dog glanced over his shoulder.

A big, black pickup pulled up to the cabin. Probably someone lost. It didn't happen often, but some people found their way up the winding gravel road to the cabin.

Mad Dog would spend a few minutes detailing the way back to the main road in the valley below. They'd comment on the view, but he wouldn't invite them to stay, and they'd be on their way.

And then he could get back to what he was doing. Which was what? Throwing himself off a cliff?

Dragging in a deep breath, he let it go on a sigh.

Two men dropped down from the truck. One of them opened the back door, and a German Shepherd leaped out onto the ground.

7

Recognition made Mad Dog's heart beat a little faster. He knew one of the guys, and automatically started walking toward them.

He picked up the pace, ignoring the sharper rocks digging into his bare feet.

The men climbed the porch and knocked on the door. They hadn't noticed him yet, coming across the rocky hillside. The dog glanced up and let out a woof.

Both men turned as one and grinned.

"Mad Dog, you old son-of-a-bitch." Hank 'Montana' Patterson hurried down the steps and across the rocks to meet him, hand outstretched.

Mad Dog gripped his hand and was pulled into a bear hug that took his breath away.

Hank pounded his back, laughing. "You don't know how hard it was to get hold of you." He stepped back and ran his gaze over Mad Dog. "You look like shit."

"Thanks." Mad Dog's lips twisted into a frown. "Great to see you, too," he said, his voice dripping sarcasm as he scratched his chin beneath the four-inches of beard that had accumulated since his retirement.

Hank turned toward the man with the German Shepherd. "You might not have met the man who actually owns this cabin. Joseph Kuntz, meet Caleb Maddox."

The other man held out his hand. "Nice to meet you, finally. My friends call me Kujo." He glanced around at the cabin. "Thanks for taking care of the place."

Mad Dog shook the man's hand. "Thanks for letting me rent it. My friends call me Mad Dog."

Kujo grinned. "As one mad dog to another, it's nice to finally meet you."

Warmth stole over Mad Dog, despite the chilly morning air.

He'd gone several months without contact from any of his old friends from SEAL Team 10. Cell phone reception was nonexistent, and the cabin didn't even have electricity or a landline.

"I was just about to make a cup of coffee," he lied. "Would you care for some?"

Both men nodded.

"Now, you're talking." Hank clapped his hands together and followed him inside. "As I said, you're a hard one to reach."

Mad Dog entered the small kitchen area, where he fired up a propane-powered camp stove and set a pot of water over the flame. When he met Kujo's gaze, he felt a moment of consternation.

"The solitude comes with the cabin," Kujo answered for him. "After a while, though, it eats at you."

The man seemed to know what was going through his mind. He nodded. "It's why I came out here in the first place."

"And the reason you'll leave," Kujo said.

Mad Dog wasn't so sure of that.

"Speaking of which," Hank pulled a coffee mug off a wooden shelf and sat at the small table. "I'd like to say I came to offer you a job, but I actually came to let you know someone else is looking for you with a potential opportunity you might want to consider."

"I'm not interested," Mad Dog replied automatically.

Hank frowned. "You haven't even heard what it is."

Mad Dog shrugged. "What kind of job can a man hold with a bum knee? I was trained to fight. I don't know anything else."

Hank's shoulders rose and fell. "Suit yourself, but you should at least find out what it entails, before you shoot down the idea." He laid a satellite phone on the table. "I've programmed in the number. All you have to do is enter it. The line is secure. Talk to the man, and see what you think."

Kujo stood and walked to the camp stove. "I'll finish making coffee, if you want to make the call outside."

Feeling a little forced to make the call, but at the same time curious, Mad Dog grabbed the satellite phone and walked back out onto the porch.

Hank was an old friend. He wouldn't be bullshitting him. He'd saved his life on more than one occasion. Mad Dog owed him at least the phone call.

He punched the SEND key and waited while the phone rang on the other end of the line.

"Maddox?" a deep, male voice answered.

"This is Maddox," he confirmed.

"This is Retired Navy Commander Greg Lambert."

Mad Dog's eyes narrowed. He'd heard of the commander, though he'd never actually met him. "Patterson said you had something you wanted to talk to me about."

"I do. I'm working on an important project and need a few good men like yourself to man it."

"I'm out of the Navy, sir. Seems they don't have

much use for broken SEALs. What good would I be to your project?"

"Can you walk?"

"I can, but I limp. I don't run as fast as I used to. Again, I don't see how I can help."

"How are your shooting skills?"

He'd brought his personal rifle and handguns with him to the cabin and fired them on a regular basis. Shooting and cleaning the weapons helped combat the boredom. "They're okay."

"I'll cut to the chase," Lambert said.

"Good, 'cause I don't want to waste your time."

"Fair enough." The commander paused and then launched in. "Our nation is in trouble. Terrorists have established sleeper cells across the country. The chatter on the internet is getting stronger, and the president is concerned. The radicals are actively recruiting and planning bigger hits. Think about the bombing at the Boston Marathon, the mass shootings in San Bernardino, California and the Orlando nightclub. Those events, and more, were performed by radicalized 'soldiers' of the Islamic State. We have to stop them before they take more innocent American lives."

"Sounds like a job for Homeland Security."

"I'd like to think they could handle it. But frankly, they don't have the training and skills needed to eradicate the threat. What my group is doing is fighting back with its own sleeper agents."

Impatient for the man to get to the point, Mad Dog frowned. "What does that have to do with me?"

"I'm getting to that. To be exact," Lambert said,

"we're fighting back as *Sleeper* SEALs. Men who, for whatever reason, have left active duty and are signing on to infiltrate areas suspected of having these insurgent cells. In effect, they're establishing sleeper cells to combat terrorism before the terrorists have the opportunity to strike."

"One-man cells?" Mad Dog asked. "Doesn't that go against everything they taught us in BUD/S? The reason why SEALs are so effective is they work, sleep and breathe as a team."

"True, and you will have communication access to our headquarters for support. However, you'd be going into an area autonomously. Alone. One thing you need to understand...these missions are not officially sanctioned by the government. We're flying under the radar —part of the CIA but not acknowledged. Because, of course, CIA is not authorized to operate on US soil."

Despite himself, Mad Dog could feel his pulse quicken, and his hand tightened on the phone. His blood hadn't moved that fast since his last mission as a SEAL. And it felt good. "Are you suggesting we take the law into our own hands?" *We.* Already, he was talking like he'd agreed to the assignment. Which he hadn't.

Lambert paused. "If anything goes south, the US government will deny all association with your efforts. You'd be on your own to bail yourself out. For the most part, you'll be on your own. Well, in this particular case, not so very much on your own."

"What do you mean?"

"Where I need you to go, and what I need you to do, will depend on one other person."

"Who? The radicalized soldier you want me to keep an eye on?"

"No. I think the radicalized soldier will find you as long as you are with the other individual."

"Who is this other person?" Mad Dog asked. "Another SEAL?"

"No," Lambert said. "An agent with the CIA."

"Assuming I accept this mission," Mad Dog said. "Who will be in charge? Your organization or the CIA?"

"Neither. The CIA agent is heading to Montana to lure the radicalized soldier to a place the agent is familiar with, and to get the terrorist away from more heavily populated areas. You will work with the agent to identify and neutralize the threat."

"And by neutralize, you mean..."

"Employ whatever means necessary to keep our country safe."

Mad Dog let that sink in for a second before asking, "What has the so-called soldier done to warrant being neutralized?"

"Have you heard of the recent bombing of our embassy in Ottawa?

"I've been out of radio, television and cell phone contact for the past two months. Fill me in."

"Two radicalized terrorists, brothers, fashioned bombs out of fertilizer and other ingredients, and set them off in front of the embassy. Nineteen people were killed, ten of them children on a field trip."

A surge of anger burned through Mad Dog. Killing adults was bad enough, but murdering children... "Why do you think these brothers will follow the CIA agent to Montana?"

"Not brothers. *Brother.* After the bombing, the agent was tasked with assassinating the brothers. The agent got one of them while they were in Toronto. From all the chatter on the internet, we know the remaining brother has sworn vengeance. Not to mention, he's already made an attempt on the operative's life. That's where you come in."

"How so?"

"Your mission will be to cover the agent's six. At the same time, you'll be on the lookout for the terrorist and remove him."

"Just one terrorist?"

"For now. As far as we know, the man is working alone, but we suspect he's recruiting additional members to his cause. Whether they're with him, or in other parts of the country, is unknown."

"Montana, then?"

"That's where the agent has gone."

Mad Dog felt a rush of adrenaline course through his body. Something he hadn't felt in a long time. "What's the agent's name? Where in Montana will I find him?"

"Jolie Richards. Head for Eagle Rock, Montana. It's a small town in the foothills of the Crazy Mountains."

"Jolie Richards." Mad Dog rolled the name on his tongue. "Strange name for a guy."

"Maybe because *she's* not a guy. Jolie Richards is a hotshot, trained assassin for the CIA. She's an expert marksman and knows her shit."

"I don't know," Mad Dog hedged. "I've never worked with a woman on a mission."

"It's all part of your cover. You two will pretend to be a couple. Agent Richards is from that area. She's heading back to her father's ranch, where she's familiar with the territory. She wants to draw her Tango away from potential collateral damage. We need you there to be her backup and to ensure the eradication of yet one more terrorist on US soil."

Mad Dog took a moment to process all Lambert had said. He'd be one of a two-man, or man-woman team, responsible for identifying and eliminating a threat to the US population. He'd have a purpose.

"Mission accepted?" Lambert queried.

With a nod he knew Lambert couldn't see, Mad Dog answered. "Mission accepted."

Holy shit, I'm back in the game.

CHAPTER 2

THE OLD HOUSE looked exactly like it had the day she'd left home to join the CIA. Sure, it needed a coat of paint and some rotten eaves and porch boards should be replaced, but the problems were all cosmetic. Maybe while she was waiting for her predator to find her, she could get the house fixed up and the Rocking R Ranch ready for sale. Why she'd held onto it all these years while she was away was beyond her.

Jolie Richards's heart squeezed tightly in her chest. She'd been home for two days and had yet to start work on anything resembling renovations to the house. Hell, she had yet to step inside, preferring to bed down in the barn.

The house and all the furniture, pictures and knick-knacks reminded her too much of all she'd lost.

Eight years ago, she'd sold all the livestock, turned off the utilities, locked the door and walked away from the only home she'd ever known.

The house wasn't a home to her anymore. Not without her father there.

She took a deep breath, stuck the key in the lock, twisted and pushed open the door. The hinge creaked as the door swung inward.

The first thing that hit her was the musty smell and dust particles stirred up by the door's movement. Sunlight through one of the windows caught the particles, giving them the appearance of a glittery fog.

Everything was as she'd left it. The sheets she'd draped over the furniture were exactly where she'd laid them. Her father's ten-point deer antler rack was mounted on the wall. He'd loved hunting and providing food for the winter that didn't come from a store. Many times, she'd thought he'd have been happiest if he'd been born a century earlier, in a time when a man raised his own food or hunted for it. He preferred to be out on his ranch, riding his favorite horse.

Which reminded Jolie, she needed to check with local ranchers and see what kind of mount she could rent, borrow or buy for the time she would be here. After sitting up for eight years, the four-wheelers her father kept in the barn probably wouldn't run. They'd need complete carburetor overhauls and new tires before they'd be serviceable.

Jolie walked into the living room. The sheets on the furniture made the lumps beneath appear ghost-like. She suspected removing them would elicit an entirely different set of ghosts—memories of sitting by the fire at her father's feet, petting one of their hounds, reading books about faraway places or playing a hand of rummy. Cold winter nights had been spent warming by the fire. During the summer, Jolie had worked at her father's side, mending fences, herding livestock and hauling hay.

She'd learned to shoot a rifle before she'd learned how to braid her hair. Had her mother lived, Jolie would have been raised differently. But her mother had passed when Jolie was only five years old. Her only memories of her mother were of her sitting by her bedside, reading books or singing in her soft, husky voice.

Jolie's father had become the center of her universe. Perhaps the five-year-old Jolie clung to him, shadowed his every footstep and refused to let him out of her sight because she was afraid of losing her only surviving parent. Whatever the reason, she'd followed her father through every aspect of ranching, farming and hunting.

By the time she was thirteen, she could shoot as well, if not more accurately, than her father. In the long run, her expert marksmanship had been what had gotten her where she wanted to be in her career with the CIA. Her skill was what now led her back to her home in Montana.

Jolie let go of the breath she'd been holding as she'd walked through the front door. She'd have to work past her memories and get on with living, or she wouldn't be ready when Abdul Nadir showed up to wreak his vengeance and claim his prize.

Her.

In the meantime, she had work to do and staring at it wouldn't get it done.

Carefully folding sheets one at a time to keep the amount of dust down in the house, she carried them out to the front porch to shake them out.

Once she had all the windows opened to let fresh air in and the dust covers removed from the living room, she moved on to her old bedroom.

Her lips twisted into a wry smile as she entered. Again, nothing had changed. She switched on the over-head light. One of the bulbs popped, but the others shone down on her full-sized bed. She pulled off the sheets, wadding the dust into them and carried them out to the porch.

Thankfully, she'd had the electricity turned on before she'd come home. She worried about whether the washing machine and dryer would work. If not, she'd have to make a trip to Eagle Rock and hope they'd built a laundromat while she'd been away. In the meantime, she had the sleeping bag she'd been using in the barn. She would use that until she had clean sheets.

At the end of her bed was the cedar chest her mother had given to her. Jolie opened it and felt the sting of tears well in her eyes. Lying on top was the quilt her mother had made for her before she'd died. She'd pieced together material from Jolie's dresses and shirts.

Jolie had loved that quilt and refused to sleep without it. Thankfully, the cedar chest had served it well, keeping critters and moths from destroying the fabric.

Lifting it out of the chest, she held it to her cheek, letting the memories wash over her. No one was there to see the tears, to witness the bad-ass CIA agent give in to the sadness threatening to overwhelm her.

She'd left Montana to escape the memories. Her return was to draw out a terrorist. While in the process of doing her job, she'd wrap up her old life and, finally, let go of her old home and ranch.

"Pardon me," a voice said behind her.

Jolie let out a shriek and spun to face the intruder. She'd been so caught up in revisiting her past, she'd forgotten to take care of her present.

She stared at a man wearing a black leather jacket, black jeans and black combat boots. Everything about him screamed strength with an underlying threat of danger.

Jolie backed a step. "Who the hell are you? And what are you doing in my house?"

He shook his head. "The door was wide open. I thought you might be in trouble, so I came in." The man stuck out his hand. "Caleb Maddox. I assume you're Jolie Richards?"

Without taking his hand, she stared at him, her eyes narrowing. "Caleb Maddox, you're trespassing. I suggest you get out of my house and off my property before I shoot you."

Instead of looking shocked or scared, the man laughed.

Jolie reached beneath her jean jacket for the handgun she had placed there in her shoulder holster.

Mad Dog held up a hand. "Seriously. You don't have to shoot me. I was sent here to help."

Her frown deepened. "With what?"

The man glanced around. "For one, getting this place into some semblance of order. Can't have you sleeping in the barn."

A pulse pounded at her temples. "How did you know I was sleeping in the barn?"

"I checked out the barn before entering the house."

She pulled the handgun from the holster and pointed it at his chest. "Why would you be checking out my barn, and then entering my house, uninvited?"

His grin broadened, and he touched the barrel of the pistol and pointed it away from his chest. "They told me you might be resistant."

Jolie shook her head and readjusted her aim to his chest. The man wasn't making sense. If she shot him, she could claim trespassing and feeling threatened. No jury in the world would question her reason for shooting. However...he was really hot with his black hair and eyes so brown they could have been black.

"I take it I'm not being clear enough." The man lowered his hand. "I'm Caleb Maddox. My friends call me Mad Dog. I'm here to provide you backup in your effort to smoke out Abdul Nadir. In effect, I'm your partner for this case."

Anger blasted through her. "The hell you are! For one: the CIA doesn't stage operations on US soil. It's not exactly legal. If Nadir shows up and attacks me while I'm here on *vacation*, I'll be forced to defend myself... and kill him. Two: I don't need anyone else involved in this effort. It just clouds the issue and my cover story."

Mad Dog opened his mouth as if to protest, but he stopped short.

Rustling beneath the bed made Jolie look away from her intruder in time to see a furry shadow race across her boots and duck into the open door of her closet.

Jolie darted backward and would have fallen into the open cedar chest.

But a hand snapped out and grabbed her flailing wrist, the one holding her pistol. Pointing the weapon upward, the man yanked her forward.

She crashed into a hard wall of muscles, the fingers on her empty hand digging into a leather jacket, holding on to get her balance.

Balance wasn't to be found with her face pressed to Mad Dog's shirt. Her senses filled with his musky after-shave and the earthy, masculine scent of leather. Mad Dog. Yeah, the name was sexier than Caleb.

Overwhelmed, confused and secretly turned on by Mad Dog's nearness, she held on for a moment, weighing her options. Accept his help and run the risk of making a fool of herself over the way the man smelled, or shoot him and deal with the local authorities with a trespassing plea.

WHEN JOLIE LOST HER BALANCE, Mad Dog had instinctively reached for her and crushed her to his chest.

Yeah, he'd grown up in a bad neighborhood, and his father hadn't taught him much in the way of right and wrong but, deep inside, he'd always known he had to protect people. Instinct had served him well on more than one occasion. Protecting his military family and friends, he'd learned he would do most anything to keep one of them from being hurt.

Since Jolie was his new partner, Mad Dog naturally extended that need to protect to her.

He had to admit, protecting a woman was different from protecting his SEAL brothers. A lot different. He'd never felt like this holding one of his buddies. Hell, he'd never held one the way he was holding Jolie. And none of them had felt quite like this woman—with a body that was lean and muscular, soft and curvy, all at once. Her strawberry-blond hair and green eyes were hard to resist, but the freckles across her pert nose sealed the deal. How could a woman who appeared so wholesome and girl-next-door be a kick-ass CIA agent? An assassin?

Fuck. This assignment was going to be harder than he'd thought.

A warm, electric current ripped through him from point of impact, his chest, all the way to his groin. Now was not the time to get a hard-on. Now was the time to establish himself as someone who could help.

Though Jolie's words had been less than inviting, he could see the tough, CIA agent's consternation at being assigned an unknown partner. He understood. It was an issue of trust. He had to earn it.

Starting with not mauling her or letting on that she was turning him on just by rubbing her body up against his.

Mad Dog set her on her feet and stepped back. The air in the room seemed to chill, and he almost regretted having to put distance between them. "Look, I'm not here to get in your way. I'm here as a second pair of eyes. You can't keep watch in all directions, all the time. I've got your six."

As she holstered her weapon, she frowned up at him. "Out of curiosity—and I'm not saying I accept this assignment of yours—just who sent you?"

He hesitated. "So, you weren't expecting me, I take it?"

Jolie crossed her arms over her chest. "No."

He nodded. "I see."

She glared. "I'm glad you see. Could you help me understand what the hell you're doing in my house?"

"Let me start over and give you a little background."

"Please."

"I'm Caleb Maddox."

"Your friends call you Mad Dog." She narrowed her eyes., "We've established that."

"I'm a former Navy SEAL."

She tilted back her head, her gaze raking over him. "How do I know that's true?"

"I could say SEALs never lie, but that might be a lie, for all you know. And well, sometimes we have to lie for the mission." He pulled out his dog tags from under his T-shirt. "I've only been out of commission for a few months. I couldn't bring myself to retire my dog tags."

She reached out and touched the dog tags and, in doing so, touched his hand.

Again, an electric current rushed through Mad Dog's body. Hell, he'd been around women. Had his share of sex when he was still on active duty. But he'd never felt anything quite like the reaction he was having toward Agent Richards.

"Maddox, Caleb." She quickly dropped her hand, as if she'd felt the current as well. "These could be cheap Chinese shit."

He tucked away the tags and chain inside his shirt. "They're government issue." He clapped his hands together. "Anyway, my new boss sent me up to help out a CIA agent—namely you—with a potentially dangerous situation." His lips twitched. "He didn't mention the problem might be critter-related."

"I don't need backup. I can take care of it myself," she said. "So, you can head back to wherever you came from."

"Colorado. I drove up today."

She raised her eyebrows. "Then back to Colorado you can go."

Rustling sounded from the closet, and the raccoon skittered back across the floor and under the bed.

Jolie edged toward him, her gaze on the floor, her hand going to the gun in the shoulder holster.

"If you insist... I'll go back to Colorado and let you handle your guest on your own." He turned as if to leave, watching her out of the corner of his eye.

She was staring at the bed, drawing her weapon. "Yeah. Don't let the door hit you in the backside on your way out," she muttered.

He paused. "Do you want me to get the critter out before I leave?"

She chewed on her bottom lip. "I really don't need help." Only she didn't sound all that certain.

Amused that an assassin looked so perturbed by a wild animal, he smothered a smile. "Look, it helps to have two people in this situation. One to scare the varmint out, the other to capture it when it comes running."

"If you say so..." She gnawed on that lip, making Mad Dog want to kiss it better. "Or I can just shoot it."

"If you want to blow a hole in the floor, inviting more of the same to enter through yet another route."

She straightened and shot him a quick glance before returning her attention to the bed. "What do you suggest?"

"How attached are you to the sheets hanging on the railing outside?"

She shrugged. "Not very."

"If you don't mind donating one to the cause, with the expectation of it being ripped to shreds, we can take care of this pretty quickly."

"Okaaay," she said.

"I'll be right back." Mad Dog ran out to the porch, snagged a sheet and hurried back into the bedroom where Jolie stood exactly where he'd left her.

"What now?" she asked.

"Move around to the other side of the bed and make noise. I'll catch the raccoon as he runs out."

It sounded simple enough, but the execution didn't come out quite like Mad Dog anticipated.

Jolie made noise, and the raccoon darted out from under the bed. Unfortunately, not in the direction Mad Dog had been prepared for.

The creature ran out the other side and headed for the open door to the bedroom.

With the sheet in hand, Mad Dog dove for the animal, hitting the floor hard on his bad knee. Pain shot through his leg. He ignored it, trapped the raccoon in the sheet and scooped it up. Figuring he only had a few seconds before the raccoon ripped through the thin sheet, Mad Dog rushed out of the bedroom and half-ran, half-limped down the hallway, holding the sheet away from his body.

The raccoon went ballistic, ripping at the sheet in a desperate attempt to get free.

"Hurry, before he gets out," Jolie said, following behind Mad Dog.

Like he didn't already know that. Mad Dog limped faster. Right as he cleared the front doorway, the raccoon tore free of the sheet.

"Close the door!" Mad Dog yelled.

Jolie slammed the screen door shut behind the man and the animal.

Mad Dog dropped the sheet. The varmint lay buried beneath, but soon worked its way free and ran to what it assumed was a tree and climbed.

The tree happened to be Mad Dog's leg.

He grabbed the creature by the scruff of the neck and tossed it toward the bushes lining the front of the deck.

Seconds later, the animal disappeared beneath the branches.

Giggling sounded behind the screen door.

Mad Dog glanced up.

Jolie held her belly around her middle, her face red, her eyes dancing.

"What's so damned funny?" he asked, though his own lips were twitching. The woman's mirth was contagious.

Jolie let go of the amusement she'd barely held in and laughed out loud. "You should have seen your face! Wish I'd filmed that raccoon climbing your leg. I... My God, I can't breathe."

A chuckle rose in his throat.

Jolie's laughter infected him, and he joined her.

Finally, she opened the door and stepped out on the deck, her grin slowly fading to a small smile. "Did he bite you? They can carry rabies."

"I know." He turned right and left, trying to inspect all the places the animal touched.

"Stand still and let me check," Jolie commanded.

With his lips still twitching, Mad Dog stood still.

Jolie circled him, studying practically every inch of his body. By the time she finished, he was fully turned on. Thankfully his jeans were snug enough to keep from showing his full attraction to her perusal.

"Other than a few scratches, I don't see anything to be concerned about."

"We need to check that room. The raccoon got into the house. If we don't find and plug the hole, it might get back in."

Jolie glanced toward the road leading up to the ranch house. "Yeah. It's getting close to dusk. We can't leave it to chance. I don't plan on sharing my bed with a raccoon."

We.

The reference wasn't lost on Mad Dog. Perhaps she wouldn't insist on him leaving quite so soon. Either that, or she was waiting until they figured out the critter problem. Then she'd boot him out the door.

Whatever her reason, it would buy him time to convince her he was an asset to her mission. And he wanted to stick around. He found he liked the tough agent and even more so, now that he'd seen her green eyes dance with laughter. The woman transformed from badass to sweet girl in seconds. He wanted to see that transformation again.

Mad Dog followed her into the house. "You should laugh more often."

Jolie snorted. "How do you know I don't?"

"By the lines on your forehead. I bet you spend most of your days frowning."

"Not that it's any concern of yours, but I don't find much to laugh about in my line of work."

"All work and no play makes you old fast."

"Says a SEAL who spent most of his service days deployed or training."

He shrugged. "We found time to laugh."

"We." She shook her head and stepped into the bedroom they'd vacated moments before. "I work alone."

"A fact you've made perfectly clear. But that was in the past. This is the present, and I'm here to help."

"Then start by helping me figure out how that raccoon got into my bedroom."

Jolie started her inspection at one corner of the room.

Mad Dog took the other end of the room. No holes in the corners or ceiling. He dropped to his haunches and looked under the bed at the same time as Jolie.

"Damn," Jolie said.

A heating vent had been pushed out of the floor, far enough to allow a persistent animal to wedge itself through the small space.

"That means the ductwork to the vent is displaced as well. Basement or crawlspace?" he asked.

"Basement."

They rose at the same time and stared at each other over the mattress.

"That means they're getting in through the basement." Jolie chewed on her lower lip. "That's where the ductwork is located."

"How long has it been since you've been here?"

She looked away. "Eight years."

"No one checked on the house and contents in that time?"

Jolie shook her head. "No. This is my first time home since—in that time." She walked to the closet, avoiding his direct stare.

Mad Dog had a feeling something had happened eight years ago. Something that made her leave. By her body language, it wasn't something she wanted to talk about to a stranger. So, he didn't push. Everyone was entitled to his or her secrets.

Jolie slid hangers across the bar. "I should have gotten rid of these old clothes eight years ago." When she glanced down at the floor of the closet, she gasped.

"What?"

The tough CIA agent dropped to her knees, her face softening.

Mad Dog stepped beside her and went down on his haunches, his heart thudding in his chest at the change in her expression.

She'd softened, her mouth curling into a smile so sweet it melted his heart.

He tore his glance away from her face and looked at what held her attention.

In a makeshift nest of old clothes and shoeboxes was a litter of raccoon kits, their eyes still closed, huddled together for warmth.

"No wonder she was so desperate to get out of the sheet," Jolie whispered. "But I can't let them live in the house."

"I'm sure if we take them outside, the mother will find them and move them somewhere safe."

Jolie looked up at him. "You think?"

"Let's see what happens," he said softly.

As appeared to be her habit when she wasn't sure, Jolie chewed on her bottom lip. "What if something else gets them?"

"We'll put them close to where the mother disappeared. We can watch out for them from the front porch."

"I know raccoons can be pests, but I can't bring myself to hurt the babies. They deserve a chance at life." A tear slipped down her cheek. "My father wouldn't kill kits, even though the adults ate chickens, stole eggs and raided the feed." Jolie reached for the nest.

"Let me. I'm already acquainted with their mother." He gave Jolie a twisted grin and lifted the entire bundle into his arms.

This time, she led the way to the door and opened it for him.

He walked out onto the porch, looking first to make sure no one else had slipped into the area while they were otherwise occupied by the animals.

When he'd ascertained the immediate vicinity posed no more of a threat than being attacked by a mother raccoon, Mad Dog carried the bundle of babies down the stairs.

Pushing his way through the overgrown bushes, he set the bundle on the ground.

"Any sign of the mother?" Jolie asked from above.

"No." He glanced up to see her leaning over the porch rail, her green eyes bright, her strawberry-blond hair falling forward around her shoulders. The woman had no clue how beautiful she was with the sun shining on her head, burnishing her light red-gold hair into copper.

Mad Dog positioned the bundle against the base of bush and tucked the clothing around the kits to keep them warm. Once he'd settled them, he rose and glanced around. "Shouldn't you be somewhere safer, considering you have a terrorist after you?"

Jolie shot a glance around the yard and fields in front of the house and shrugged. "I'm keeping watch."

"Yeah, well, I'd feel better if you went back inside."

Her eyebrows drew together. "I've been with the CIA for the past eight years, and I'm still alive."

"How many of those eight years have you had a terrorist targeting you?"

CHAPTER 3

JOLIE WANTED to be angry at the man standing in her yard, but she couldn't. He'd just shown a softer, compassionate side of himself by capturing the mother raccoon and releasing her outside. And if that wasn't enough to convince her he couldn't be all bad, he'd relocated the kits so the mother raccoon could find them.

She sighed. "None. I haven't had a single terrorist targeting me. I'm usually shooting from a semi-protected position. My targets never know what hit them."

He nodded. "Until now."

"Until now," she agreed. "Somehow, Abdul Nadir, formerly known as Dwayne Duncan, learned who took out his brother. I think the guy is a computer hacker or knows someone who is. Anyway, my contacts back in Virginia on the cyber team tell me Dwayne is online and spewing threats."

"I'll check with my sources and get an update."

"Your sources?" she asked. "I thought *your* sources were *my* sources. You *are* working with the CIA, aren't you?"

He stared straight into her eyes and answered, "If I told you..." Mad Dog's lips twitched. "Well, you get the picture."

"You'd have to kill me." She rested her hands on her hips. "Don't tempt me."

He climbed the stairs, favoring one of his legs. When he was standing beside her, he waved toward the door. "Humor me, will ya? Step inside, out of target range."

"I will, but only because I need to shore up the basement against other varmint intruders." She poked a finger toward him. "Not because you told me to."

He tipped his head. "So noted."

She entered the house, fully conscious of the man following her.

He was a big guy with broad shoulders, a trim waist and massive thighs. Though he walked with a limp, he exuded sheer masculinity, strength and confidence in every movement. And the dark stubble on his chin made her want to rub her hand across it to see just how bristly it was. She wondered how the prickly hairs would feel brushing across her naked skin.

As soon as the thought surfaced, she pushed it to the back of her mind, reminding herself that he was cramping her style. Jolie worked alone. It was easier that way. On the rare occasion she was assigned a partner, she kept him at a distance. No emotional connections. She'd learned with her family that getting emotionally involved was painful. Especially when you lost a person to death. And getting involved with another agent would be setting herself up for heartache.

Jolie headed for the basement. What better way to ground herself than by going underground to determine the extent of infestation in her old home? Her father would be appalled. He'd always taken such good care of their home.

Her mother had adored the stone and cedar exterior of the house and had decorated the interior with love and happiness in a homey rustic style, using handmade pillows and quilts, sturdy leather sofas and recliners. She'd known her husband would be coming in from a hard day's work on the ranch and hadn't wanted him to have to shower before he could relax in his recliner.

Jolie could remember sitting at her mother's feet on one of the rag rugs she'd made of coiled swatches of fabric. Before Jolie left home, she'd rolled up that rug and encased it in plastic sheeting to protect it from damage. Maybe she'd get it out while she was there.

The basement door was located near the kitchen. Jolie switched on the light, once again, grateful she'd had the forethought to have the electric company turn on the power before she'd arrived.

The light overhead burned a dull yellow and flickered. She'd check the stash of bulbs in the pantry and see if they were any good after sitting dormant for eight years. She didn't see any reason why they wouldn't be.

Before she could take the first step down, Mad Dog touched her arm.

An electric current rippled across her nerves and

coiled low in her belly. Having this man around could prove to be too much of a distraction.

"Let me go first," he said and brushed past her.

It rankled that he didn't think she could take care of herself. Then again, they were dealing with animals, not people. Why not let the man handle the creepy, crawling things that could go bump in the night while she slept?

Jolie stepped back and waved her hand. "By all means."

Mad Dog descended the stairs into the full basement. A couple of the lights weren't working, giving the entire space an eerie, shadowy aura that sent chills across Jolie's skin.

She shrugged it off. The basement was a good ten degrees cooler than the rest of the house.

By the time Jolie reached the bottom step, Mad Dog had made a complete circuit of the space.

"Clear," he pronounced.

"Clear of what?"

"Bad guys."

She snorted. "What about bad rodents?"

"We need to give it a more thorough investigation. I noticed droppings in the western corner and a small window with a broken pane. I suspect the creatures are getting in through there."

Covering every inch of the space together, they returned to the western end of the basement. The small window, emitting a scant amount of light through the broken, dirty pane, had a hole large enough for a raccoon to enter.

"If that little hole let a raccoon in, no telling what else has taken up residence," Mad Dog said.

Jolie shivered. "Great. I know I won't be sleeping tonight. I think we had mousetraps stored in the barn. I have a jar of peanut butter in my supplies."

Mad Dog nodded toward a stack of lumber. "If you don't mind my using some of that scrap lumber, I'll board up the window."

"Knock yourself out." She eyed the ductwork that had come loose. Jolie suspected it was the route the mama raccoon had taken up into her bedroom. "I'll have to have an air conditioning and heating service come out to clean the ductwork. In the meantime, I'm not turning on a fan, heater or the AC."

"Smart idea. Will you be warm enough without the heat?"

"I like sleeping cool. If it gets too cold, I can start a fire in the fireplace."

"*After* we clean the flue." He shook his head. "The last thing you want is to set the house on fire because birds have built eight years of nests in your chimney."

"Right." Jolie could kick herself. She knew all that. But she was a bit rusty, having lived in apartments since she'd left home. Maintenance had been someone else's responsibility. "I can handle the flue if you don't mind boarding the window."

"No way." Mad Dog crossed his arms over his chest. "Number one, you'd be an easy target on top of the roof. Number two, I wouldn't know if you fell off the roof while I was down here working." He lifted a board. "Tell you what—you help me here, and I'll help with the chimney."

Jolie wanted to put space between herself and the SEAL, but he was right.

He shot her a sideways glance. "You know I'm right."

"Yeah," she said. "But I don't have to like it."

His chuckle warmed the chilly basement air.

Another reason for her to put distance between them. The smoky sound of his laughter ignited a fire low in her belly. She hadn't been that aware of a man in a very long time. If ever.

"I'll need a pencil, measuring tape, hammer, nails and a saw." Mad Dog sorted through the stack of lumber and selected a board large enough to cover the broken window. "If you have it, I'd prefer an electric saw, but if you don't have one of those, the old-fashioned kind will do."

Jolie hurried to her father's workbench and opened cabinet drawers and doors until she'd located the electric saw, measuring tape, pencil, hammer and nails.

By the time she returned, Mad Dog had positioned a couple of sawhorses and laid the board across them.

Jolie plugged in the circular saw and set it down on the board beside Mad Dog.

"Thanks." He measured the window, marked the board and cut what he needed. He handed the nails to Jolie. "Do you want to do the honors?"

She shook her head, refusing to take the nails. "You're doing great. I'll let you." While he hammered the board into the window frame, she replaced the saw and the measuring tape in the cabinet, running her hand across the workbench.

She didn't realize Mad Dog had finished until he reached around her to hang the hammer on the peg board over the bench. In the process, his chest touched her back.

Holy hell, he was warm, sexy and entirely larger than life. How would she ignore a guy like that?

"Was this your workbench?" he asked.

Jolie's eyes stung. "It was my father's. During the winter, when it was too cold to be outside for long, he'd come down here and make furniture or fix farm implements." She swallowed the lump in her throat and ran her hand along the array of tools hanging on the pegboard. "He believed in every tool having a place and, when they weren't in use, the tools would be in their places."

"Sounds like an organized man." Mad Dog laid a hand on her shoulder. "You must miss him."

She nodded, that knot in her throat threatening to keep her from breathing. Again, she swallowed hard. "I couldn't stay," she whispered. "Not after he'd gone."

"Is that why you left eight years ago?" he asked, his hand still on her arm, making her feel oddly comforted and tense at the same time.

She nodded. "Eight years is a long time. You'd think I'd be over it."

"Some things you never get over." His tone had taken on a harsher tone, and he dropped his hand to his side.

When Jolie looked up at Mad Dog's face, it had hardened, his jaw appearing to be set in stone. "Did you lose someone you loved?"

Mad Dog snorted. "I lost someone. But I can't say any love was lost between us." He turned away. "Any idea where your father might have kept the chimney broom?"

She wondered who Mad Dog had lost, and why there was no love between them. Was it a parent? Or a spouse? Jolie led him to another part of the basement where a storage cabinet stood. Inside the cabinet were larger tools hanging from hooks. She selected the chimney brush and closed the cabinet.

"There should be a ladder hanging in the barn," she said. "We'll need it to get onto the roof."

Mad Dog led the way up the stairs and toward the exit. He stood in front of the doorway, blocking her exit until he declared the coast was clear.

She let out a huff of breath. "I'm a trained agent. I know how to look for danger," she muttered, finally stepping across the threshold and out onto the porch.

"Humor me," the SEAL said. "I have to justify my job." Then he winked and set off across the yard toward the barn.

"See? You agree. I don't need a bodyguard."

"No, you don't." He stopped long enough to turn and face her. "But you need a partner to have your back." He glanced over her shoulder. "Look out now—someone's coming."

She crossed her arms over her chest. "You're testing me, right?"

"No, really." He nodded toward the road.

Jolie spun, dropped to a kneeling position, and drew her gun from the shoulder holster, all in a matter of seconds.

Mad Dog stepped in front of her.

"What are you doing?" she asked.

"Taking a bullet for you, darlin'," he said.

"A bullet in the back, if you're not careful," she groused and rose, tucking the hand with the gun beneath her jacket. "It's a pickup. Most likely someone from a neighboring ranch."

The truck pulled to a stop in front of the house. A man and a woman got out. The woman reached into the truck and brought out a casserole dish, holding it with oven mitts.

Jolie chuckled. "They look really dangerous."

"You never know," Mad Dog said. "Most serial killers were mild-mannered pillars of their communities."

"I know these people. They own the ranch to the south." Jolie holstered her weapon and stepped around Mad Dog. "Tom and Sherry, it's so nice to see you."

Tom reached her first and held out his hand. "Jolie, you should have let us know you were coming. Sherry and I would have been out here sooner."

Jolie took his hand. Instead of shaking it, he pulled her into a hug.

"We missed having the Richards next door." Tom patted her back and released her.

"We heard from Mia at Bartlett's Hardware that you were back in town," Sherry said. "I brought a 'welcome home' casserole for you. I can't imagine you've had time to fix up the kitchen to cook."

"Thank you so much." Jolie waved a hand toward the house. "You're right. I just started to clean up the living area and bedroom. I haven't made it to the kitchen yet. You're welcome to come in, but I have to warn you, it's a mess."

"We don't want to keep you." Sherry headed for the porch. "I'll put this in the kitchen." The woman disappeared into the house.

"Do you need our help setting the house in order?" Tom asked, nodding toward the chimney brush.

"Thank you for the offer, but we can manage." Jolie didn't want anyone else near her place. She'd come to Montana to lure a terrorist away from populated areas. She didn't want her neighbors to become collateral damage in a radicalized jihadist's vendetta.

Tom glanced past her to Mad Dog.

Jolie turned toward the SEAL. "I'm sorry, I seem to have lost my manners. Tom Lewis, this is Caleb Maddox, my..."

"Fiancé." Mad Dog slid an arm around Jolie's waist and extended his other hand to Tom. "Jolie and I are engaged."

Jolie stiffened inside the circle of his arm.

Tom shook Mad Dog's hand and glanced from the SEAL to Jolie. "Is that so?"

"Is what so?" Tom's wife emerged on the porch, carrying the oven mitts in one hand.

"Sherry, come meet Caleb, Jolie's fiancé," Tom said.

Sherry's eyes narrowed, and then her eyebrows rose. "Her fiancé? Well, that's news. When did this happen?"

Jolie's cheeks reddened. "It was kind of sudden," she

said through gritted teeth, forcing a smile. "I've barely had time to process it." Why the hell had the SEAL blurted out they were engaged?

"It was very sudden," Mad Dog added.

"Congratulations, Jolie." Sherry held out her hand. "Show me the ring."

Jolie clutched her hands together.

"It's being sized," Mad Dog said. "We'll be sure to show you when it comes back from the jeweler's in Bozeman."

"Oh, I see. Well, still, it's so nice to see you back, and with a fiancé. What a wonderful surprise." Sherry looked from Jolie to Mad Dog. "Are you staying? Will you be living here?"

"No," Jolie said.

"Yes," Mad Dog said at the same time and laughed. "We're still discussing options." He hugged her to him. "Aren't we, dear?"

"Yes, dear," she replied, the smile hurting her cheeks.

"I've been checking the fences on your place since I've been running my cattle in your pastures." Tom waved toward the pastures. "Let me know when you need them off. I can round them up whenever you say the word."

"No hurry. It'll be a while before I run cattle again, although I am looking for a horse, so I can check the fences myself."

Tom smiled. "I'll bring two over tomorrow. Will that be soon enough?"

"Why don't you let us come over and get them?" Mad Dog said.

"Right." Tom smiled. "You two will want to choose your mounts. I have four you can pick from."

"Thank you, Tom." Jolie turned to Sherry. "I'll bring your dish back when we come."

"No hurry on the dish. I hope you like chicken and rice casserole."

"I'm sure we will." Mad Dog smiled at the woman. "Thank you for bringing it."

Sherry blushed and stammered. "We'll s-see you tomorrow, then. Come on, Tom. Leave the two love-birds alone."

Tom didn't seem as eager to leave but smiled at his wife's command. "We're glad to see you home, Jolie. Your father was a good man."

Jolie's eyes burned, but she held back the tears threatening to fall. "Thank you, Tom. He thought a lot of your family. I want to catch up on your son. Did he go to college? And your folks. Are they still in Florida?"

Tom nodded. "I'll fill you in tomorrow. Let us know if you need anything." He climbed into his truck, tipped his hat and drove out of the yard.

Jolie waited until the Lewises were out of the yard, and then she turned on Mad Dog. "Why the hell—"

He placed a finger over her mouth and leaned close. "We should get that chimney cleaned before dark."

The touch of his finger to her lips made her nerves jump and her body flush with warmth. She had to catch herself to keep from puckering and, *God forbid*, kissing that finger.

Heat suffused her cheeks, but she didn't have time to

be embarrassed, because the next thing she knew, Mad Dog was dragging her by the hand toward the barn.

Once inside, Mad Dog paused. "Ladder?"

"Hanging on the far wall." Jolie pointed.

Mad Dog handed her the flue broom, snagged the ladder from the wall and stepped back out into the late afternoon sunshine.

"Don't think you're going to get away without an explanation," Jolie warned.

"I'm sorry," he said. "Did I not tell you?"

"Tell me what?"

He grinned. "I do things for a reason, but I don't always explain myself."

Jolie snorted. "Well, you better start now. Why did you tell them that you are my fiancé?"

"I'll break my rule this once." He sighed. "We needed a cover story."

"I had one. You're the one who didn't."

"True. So, I came up with one." He puffed out his chest. "I think it works quite well."

"Yeah, well don't think you're staying in the house. I'm still not sure I trust you."

"After saving you from a potentially rabid raccoon, risking my life, you still don't trust me?" He shook his head. "Woman, you're a tough nut to crack."

Jolie chuckled. "Fine. I trust you to take care of varmints. But you're still staying in the barn."

"I guess I have my work cut out for me." He glanced around the yard and out to the tree line. "Come on, I don't like standing still for long. It gives snipers too much time to lock in." He carried the ladder to the house, propped it against the eaves and reached for the broom.

She held it away from his grasp. "You took care of the basement, I'll take care of the chimney. That was the deal."

All humor melted from his face, and his lips thinned. "On top of a roof, you're an even easier target than on the ground. Let me do this."

She hesitated, unused to having someone else doing the dirty work. But he was right. On the roof, she'd provide a distinct silhouette. "I'm not afraid of getting dirty. My father insisted I do everything he could."

"Sounds like he was pretty hard on you."

She shook her head. "Not at all. He was determined to teach me everything he knew. I think he expected me to run the ranch when he was gone." She glanced away. "I don't think even he expected to be gone so soon."

"What happened to him?"

Her lips pressed into a thin line. "He was shot while out hunting."

"Accident?"

Jolie returned her gaze to Mad Dog, her jaw tightening. "If it was an accident, whoever shot him never owned up to doing it."

"And he was never caught." Mad Dog's words weren't a question. His gaze studied her face. "You weren't interested in running the ranch?"

"Not without my father. He was the life in this place. With him gone, I couldn't do it. I'd already applied to join the CIA, expecting to be gone for several years before returning to help my father as he grew older."

She shrugged. "Plans change. People change. I couldn't stay."

"What happened to the livestock?"

"I sold everything that breathed. Horses, cattle, pigs, chickens. I didn't have the time to auction off the farm implements. They're in the barn. I imagine the rats and mice have eaten through cables. We had a tractor, a couple of ATVs and a truck. It would be nice if the truck worked. I'll need something to haul hay and feed to the barn for the horses we're borrowing from Tom. But for now, I need to keep the house from burning down." She nodded toward the ladder. "If you're going up, I'll go inside and make sure whatever you shake loose isn't alive and running loose inside."

"Good idea." He took the brush from her and started up the ladder.

"Ever cleaned a chimney before?"

Mad Dog chuckled. "Can't say that I have."

"Maybe I should do that after all," Jolie said.

"How hard can it be?" He tipped his head toward the house. "Go make sure I'm not making a disaster of the interior."

"Okay. Yell, if you need me outside to pick you up off the ground." She waited until he was on the roof then she entered the house, a smile quirking the corners of her lips. She hoped he didn't fall off the roof. He was far too good-looking to die on her watch.

Jolie gave herself a firm shake.

Don't get used to having him around. He's hired help and will be leaving as soon as the threat is gone.

The thought depressed her, but she pushed on.

CHAPTER 4

AFTER CLEANING THE CHIMNEY, Mad Dog stored the broom where it belonged in the basement, adjusted the heating ductwork to close the gap and secured it with duct tape. Then he loaded the mouse traps with peanut butter and set them out around the basement. He could hear Jolie banging around in the kitchen.

By the time he climbed the stairs, she had the kitchen clean and two place settings on the table with the casserole between them.

"Hungry?" Jolie asked.

"Starving," he said, patting his flat belly. He glanced around the kitchen. Everything appeared dust-free and shiny. "You've been busy. Very domestic."

She snorted. "Don't think that's normal for me. I'm much better at the outdoors stuff. I don't much care for cooking."

"Lucky for you, I learned how to cook at a young age." He didn't tell her it was out of self-preservation.

Nor did he tell her his earlier meals were made of whatever he could scrounge in the cabinet. His father usually drank his paycheck, forgetting he had a son at home to feed.

Mad Dog had mowed lawns and cleaned gutters for extra money to put food on the table. His dad had never showed him how to do anything, and he'd never thanked him for cooking or cleaning.

As soon as Mad Dog finished high school, he'd joined the military to get the hell away from his worthless father.

His father never once wrote him a letter or called him after he left home. The man had left nothing for his son, unless one counted all the bad memories that would fade, but never quite go away.

"My mother cooked wonderful meals before she died." Jolie smiled wryly. "I didn't get that gene." She glanced across the table at him. "What was your family like?"

"Typical," he said, without elaborating. What good did it do to dredge up his crummy past?

"Did your mother cook?"

"I don't know. She was gone by the time I turned five."

"Did she die of cancer, too?" Jolie asked softly.

Mad Dog snorted. "No. One day she was there, the next, she was gone. She gave no reason, just packed her bags and left."

"That's awful."

He shrugged. "I really didn't know her."

"At least you had your father," Jolie said. "Is he still

alive?"

"No." Mad Dog stared at the casserole, praying his partner would cease her questioning.

"Was he the cook?" Jolie persisted.

"No," he said, through gritted teeth.

Jolie studied him for a long moment. "I get it; you don't want to talk about your parents." She served up a portion of the chicken and rice onto his plate, and then scooped an equal portion onto hers. "Why?"

"Why what?"

"Why don't you want to talk about your family?"

His chest tightened, and his hands balled into fists. He hadn't thought much about his parents until he'd seen how much it hurt Jolie to talk about hers. "You had a good relationship with your family. Leave it there."

"And you didn't." She reached across the table and touched his fist. "I'm sorry."

"For what?" Mad Dog jerked back his hand. "My father was the bastard. I understand why mother left."

"But you never understood how she could leave you with him, did you?"

God, she'd hit the nail on the head. He drew a deep breath. "It doesn't matter. I survived long enough to get out."

For a moment she was blessedly silent, then, "Go ahead." She nodded toward the food on his plate. "I promise not to grill you with any more questions while you eat."

Mad Dog stared down at his plate without seeing the food. His memories took him back to that ratty trailer in the roughest neighborhood of Houston. The place his father had called home. He was lucky to be alive, considering the number of drive-by shootings and fights involving knives and handguns that had taken place around his house. He'd been in a few fistfights and had disarmed a guy with a blade, but he hadn't thought he'd ever get out of that hellhole, not until the judge made him choose.

"Caleb, you need to eat," Jolie said softly. "I'm sorry I brought up all that crap about your family. But you're here now. Fuel your body. We might be in for a helluva week."

Mad Dog glanced up into Jolie's gaze. No one had called him Caleb in a long time. It was Maddox or Mad Dog. Calling him Caleb made it sound so intimate and personal.

Not that she was getting intimate with him, but he liked the way she said his name in her warm, husky voice.

He dug his fork into the casserole and lifted it. "Here's to finding our terrorist and putting an end to his shit."

Jolie nodded and lifted a forkful of food. "To what you said. Let's get the bastard."

Before he gets us, Mad Dog thought.

After they polished off plates full of the delicious casserole, Jolie scraped the remaining food into a plastic container she'd found and cleaned earlier. Then she stood at the sink, filling it with water and soap.

Mad Dog carried his plate to the sink. "You cooked. I'll clean."

"I didn't cook," she reminded him.

"Well, you cleaned the plates we ate off. The least I can do is clean them again."

"I was going to do the rest of the dishes in the cabinet. You don't need to hang around while I do that." She took his plate, rinsed it in the empty sink then dropped it into the soapy sink.

"Fine. But it'll go much faster if I wash and you dry."

"Okay. But *I'll* wash and *you* can dry."

He took the towel she'd used earlier and assumed a position beside her.

One by one, she cleaned the dishes, and he dried. When they got to the glasses, she washed out the cabinet above and to her left.

Every time Mad Dog dried a glass, he reached around her and set it on the shelf. And every time he did, he bumped into her.

The longer they worked, the more he collided with Jolie's body, and the hotter he got. When they finally finished, Jolie popped the plug from the drain. "Well, that's all for now. I think I'll see if the water is hot enough for a real shower."

Mad Dog had just placed the last glass onto the shelf, when she turned and ran smack into him.

"Oh, sorry," she said, her gaze focused on his chest, her cheeks suffused with a pretty flush of pink.

He gripped her arms to steady her. "Let me dry your hands." He let go of her arms, took her hands in the dishtowel, and gently dried the droplets of moisture from her skin.

"No, really...you don't have to..." Her voice faded

off, and she looked up into his eyes. "This isn't going to work."

"No?" Though her hands were already quite dry, he couldn't bring himself to relinquish his hold.

And she wasn't fighting to be free.

She turned her head slowly back and forth. "There's something going on between us, and it's not right."

"Or is it too right, and you don't know how to feel about it?" Because that was the way he felt at that exact moment.

"You're my partner for this mission. Nothing else." Her fingers squeezed his, and she pulled her hands free. "As soon as we get our man, I'm out of here."

"I understand," Mad Dog said. "No strings."

"No strings and no anything else." She walked away, but then turned back. "There's a sleeping bag in the barn. That's where you can bunk."

"No way. If Nadir or Dwayne, or whoever he is, shows up, and I'm a hundred yards away, I'm doing you no good whatsoever."

"I told you. I can take care of myself."

He closed the distance between them and grabbed her arms. "Sweetheart, if someone wants you dead, you might not have a chance to take care of yourself. You need help."

Jolie inhaled and exhaled, taking her time. "You're not sleeping in the house. If you don't want to freeze to death, you'll sleep in the barn."

With that, she left him standing in the kitchen.

"Be sure to lock the door behind me, as well as the deadbolts. I'll make rounds before I leave."

She waved a hand behind her. "I'm getting a shower. If you want one, you'll have to wait."

"That'll give me time to check all the windows and doors."

She didn't respond. Nor did Mad Dog expect her to. He made his rounds of the house, checking the locks on the windows, amazed at how many were unlocked.

"They probably leave their keys in the cars, too," he muttered. That kind of lifestyle was completely foreign to his, having grown up in one of the most desperate neighborhoods. If someone left a door unlocked, someone else would find it, walk in and take whatever the hell he wanted.

Checking the locks took longer than he'd expected, but it helped also to pass the time. He wanted a shower after working in the dusty basement and carrying the frantic raccoon out of the house.

While Jolie showered, Mad Dog walked out to his truck and collected his Go Bag. Sadly, it contained all of his worldly goods. He'd rented the cabin in the mountains fully furnished. When he'd left his apartment in Virginia, he'd sold or donated all of his furniture and electronics. Nothing tied him down. Especially not things. And he didn't have anyone to go home to or who cared whether or not he lived or died.

Well, there was his SEAL team. They'd tried to keep in touch up until he'd moved to Colorado to the remote cabin with no cell phone reception.

When he'd become a SEAL, his confidence as a man had soared. He'd even begun to think that once the missions slowed down, he might have a shot at a real life, a relationship with a woman. Children weren't completely out of the question, though he worried he'd be too much like his father. In which case, he'd rather not bring children into a world where they weren't loved.

Darkness had fallen on Montana while they'd eaten their dinner. Outside, the stars shone like so many twinkly lights. He'd seen skies as clear and beautiful in Colorado.

For a couple minutes, he stood out in the open, locating some familiar constellations. If he stayed in Montana long, he'd invest in a decent telescope.

It was just a dream. Once this mission was complete, he'd be assigned to another. And he had no idea where that one might take him. He'd be better off sticking with just his Go Bag and his pickup.

As much as he tried to steer clear of the woman, his thoughts went to the CIA agent showering in the house. Under her tough exterior, her body was all female. And he'd bet her skin was silky soft and beautiful with the water running over her naked body.

Against his better judgment, he'd stood beside her washing dishes, and touched her more than was necessary. His body had felt drawn to her like a moth to flame. If he wasn't careful, he'd be scorched. Or she might shoot him.

His lips twitched. From what Lambert had told him, Jolie Richards was an expert marksman and sniper. She knew her way around weapons and wasn't afraid to pull the trigger.

He'd be smart to keep his hands off Agent Richards

and his mind on what was more important—keeping her alive and *neutralizing* a terrorist.

With his bag in hand, he entered the house and locked the door behind him.

"Shower's yours," Jolie called out, and a door closed with a snick.

Mad Dog walked down the hall to the open bathroom. The air was warm and moist and smelled of honeysuckle.

The scent reminded him of the vines on the fence behind the trailer park where he'd grown up. For him, honeysuckle was a symbol of hope. No matter how many times the park manager had cut it, the hardy plant grew back. No matter how many times his father had physically or verbally abused him, cutting him down, making him feel small and stupid, Mad Dog had fought his way back.

He liked that Jolie used honeysuckle shampoo.

Closing the door, he inhaled deeply and closed his eyes. The woman was even more tempting than before. He really needed to rein in his lusty desires and keep focused on the task.

After a quick, cold shower, he dressed in jeans and a sweatshirt, figuring the night would be cold and the sleeping bag might not be enough.

Pulling on his boots, he gathered his bag and carried it into the living room where he stashed it in the corner.

The room still needed a thorough cleaning and dusting, but the musty smell did nothing to hide the fact this had once been a cozy place to hang out when the weather was too cold to go outside.

He could picture Jolie sitting here with her father, enjoying a television program or listening to music.

Her father had made a home for her, teaching her skills she'd need to survive on her own. Despite losing her mother, she'd had it good, with a loving parent there for her every step of her childhood.

He wondered if he should let her know that he was heading out to the barn. Mad Dog walked to the room he'd found her in earlier that day, the one that had housed the raccoon, and stood listening, trying to ascertain whether she'd already gone to bed.

With his hand raised to knock, he paused.

The door opened, and Jolie gasped. "Oh."

He lowered his hand. "I'm heading out to the barn. That is, unless you've changed your mind and want me to stay in the house."

She drew her bottom lip between her teeth and chewed on it, a frown denting her brown. She wore an old, oversized Denver Broncos T-shirt that hung halfway down her thighs and nothing else that he could see. Her nipples' tight little nubs pressed against the soft fabric.

Jolie wrapped her arms around herself and shook her head. "No, you should probably go. I'll lock the door behind you."

"Good. And if you hear anything or are worried, just yell really loudly. I might hear you."

"Thanks," she said, her tone flat, her lips twisting. "You've made your point. I'll sleep with my Glock on my nightstand. There, are you happy?"

"I'd be happier closer to you, but that helps." He

touched a finger to her cheek. "I'm not trying to be a pest, but I want to keep you safe until we get our man."

She nodded. "I get it. What you don't understand is that I came out here to get away from others. I don't want anyone else caught in the crossfire. No collateral damage."

"I'm used to taking risks. It goes with the job description." He rubbed his thumb across her bottom lip. "Goodnight, Jolie. I hope you sleep well."

Then he left her standing there and walked out the front door, pulling it closed behind him. He waited there until he heard the metallic click of the deadbolt shooting into place.

"Goodnight, Caleb," she said, her voice muffled by the sturdy wooden door.

With a smile tugging at his lips, he clicked on his flashlight and walked across the yard to the barn.

Once inside, he found a light switch and turned it on. A dull yellow bulb hung from the ceiling, casting a soft glow into the center of the old structure. It smelled of really old hay and dust.

Mad Dog entered what must have been the tack room in which Jolie had slept the previous nights. An old Army cot stood in one corner with a sleeping bag rolled at the foot.

He unrolled the bag and lay down on top of it. After sunset, the temperature had dropped at least twenty degrees, but his sweatshirt was keeping him warm for the moment. A hint of honeysuckle clung to the sleeping bag.

The thought that Jolie had slept in the bag recently, made him warm all over.

And she was in the house all alone. If a terrorist really wanted to get to her, he could break a window.

Mad Dog cocked his head and listened. He could hear nothing outside the walls of the barn. How was he supposed to protect his partner if he was half a football field away from her? Hell, he wouldn't hear if she screamed. Not through the walls of the house and the barn.

He gathered the sleeping bag, pressed it to his nose and inhaled the scent of honeysuckle.

A minute later, he was out of the tack room, the barn, and standing at the base of the porch stairs before he could change his mind. Not that he would.

He crept up the stairs, wedged himself and the sleeping bag into a corner and lowered himself into the cocoon, guessing the temperature would dip close to freezing by morning. Already, every breath he released produced a cloud of vapor.

Wrapping the bag around himself, but keeping his feet free so he could jump up if necessary, he laid his handgun beside his leg and tried to close his eyes.

So much had changed in the past forty-eight hours, he doubted he'd sleep. He was too wound up to even consider closing his eyes.

From contemplating self-destruction to partnering with a trained assassin, he'd come a long way, physically and mentally, in a very short time.

He was just glad he had work that required the skills he'd trained so hard to gain.

That Jolie didn't want a partner didn't hurt his feelings. He could understand her reticence. She liked to work alone. Mad Dog would have to convince her a partner would be a benefit. Not just for varmint removal of the four-legged variety.

He grinned in the darkness. First day on the job and he'd wrestled a raccoon. The guys from his old team would have a good laugh at his expense.

It had been a long time since he'd had a good laugh at himself. And even longer since he'd been attracted to a woman enough to want to stick around.

He lifted the corner of the sleeping bag and sniffed again.

Oh, yeah. He wasn't ready to abandon this project. Not yet.

CHAPTER 5

BEFORE TAKING HER SHOWER, Jolie had cleaned out her bedroom and closet of all the animal droppings, shredded fabric and papers the raccoon had used in forming her nest.

No matter how much she'd cleaned, mopped and dusted, she still had an itchy, twitchy feeling when she laid in her bed.

Maybe she'd feel better once the HVAC man came to decontaminate the heating and air-conditioning vents.

Every little noise, from the creaking of the house as it settled, to the rustle of trees outside, sounded like little raccoon or mouse feet skittering across Jolie's nerves.

For a badass sniper and assassin, she wasn't so good at handling animals. The handgun on her nightstand gave her a little comfort. But, like Mad Dog had said, if she shot at a rat or raccoon, she'd likely put a hole in the flooring, giving them one more way to access her room.

For an hour, she lay staring at the ceiling. Yes, it was her old bedroom where she'd grown up. Yes, it still had the same paintings on the wall and her mother's quilt on the bed. But it was different.

The entire house was different. Her father wasn't down the hall snoring softly. He wouldn't be rising early in the morning to go out and milk the cow, or feed the hogs and chickens. He wouldn't be there like he had when she'd made scrambled eggs and bacon for breakfast.

Her eyes burned and tears welled, spilling out the corners. After so many years, she'd thought her heart would have healed. Coming back to her old home had only ripped open the wound. She missed her father. Her only family.

The walls seemed to close in around her, and her breathing became more difficult.

Jolie tossed back the quilt, grabbed a jacket and padded barefooted down the hallway. She didn't bother to put on pants, her T-shirt was long enough to cover everything that counted, and she really didn't give a damn what anyone thought about how she was dressed. All she knew was she needed to get out of the house before she suffocated.

She struggled with the deadbolt, her hands shaking as it finally released and she could pull open the door.

Cool air hit her face and legs. Pushing through the screen door, she stepped out onto the porch. Her feet welcomed the chill of the boards against her skin.

Jolie drank in deep breaths of the clear, mountain air. When she'd been a teen, hormonal and thickheaded, she'd step out on the porch at night to clear her thoughts.

Something about the crispness of the stars and the sharpness of the air she breathed brought her back to calm. This time was no different.

She stared out at the plethora of sparkling stars in the sky, picking out the easy constellations, without even trying. Some things never changed, and she found solace in that.

Her father had been a very busy man, tending to a ranch with cattle, horses and other livestock. He rarely had time to relax. But he made time to take her stargazing. He'd been fascinated by the vastness of the universe and shared his fascination and knowledge with his only child.

Tears fell in earnest now—a silent cleansing she never realized she'd needed until now. After her father had been killed, she'd set about selling every living thing on the ranch. Anything that required her to stay and care for it, had to go. The pain had been so excruciating, she'd hurried through the motions, intent on getting away, thinking the pain would lessen once she left.

In a way, leaving had helped dull the pain. But it was still there. The hollowness of being truly alone in the world. The loss of her mother had hit her hard. She'd clung to her father for the love and support she knew he'd provide. Never in all her years had she ever thought she'd lose him, too.

When he'd died, something inside her had died with him. The ability to love someone else. Why bother falling in love, when something as random as a freak hunting accident, an automobile wreck or illness could take that person away. One day he could be there, the next day gone. Forever.

Jolie sat on the top step of the porch, wrapped her arms around her bare legs and let the tears fall. She hadn't bothered to slip the jacket over her shoulders and didn't notice the cold, at first.

Sobs pushed up from her lungs, but she swallowed them, trying not to make enough noise to wake the man in the barn. CIA assassins didn't cry. But she needed this. Needed the release and needed it to be without witnesses.

At first, she allowed the tears to flow unheeded, dripping down on her knees drawn up under her T-shirt and pressed up against her chest. When her shirt became damp, it absorbed the cold and made her shiver.

Jolie rubbed her hands down her face in an attempt to slow the flow of tears. Her body shook as cold sank through her skin and into her bones.

She blindly reached for her jacket, and it magically dropped down over her shoulders, at first cool, then warming.

An arm slipped around her and pulled her against a warm, solid body.

Jolie glanced up, too buried in her grief to be alarmed when she looked into Mad Dog's face, bathed in starlight. She stiffened against him and ducked her head. "I'm sorry. You weren't supposed to see this." When she tried halfheartedly to pull away, he tightened his arm around her.

"It's okay. I won't tell a soul."

"It's just..." She swallowed hard, the lump in her throat refusing to allow the words to escape.

"You don't have to explain yourself. Just let me keep you warm for now," he said. "You're shaking like a leaf."

She hadn't realized when she'd started to tremble or why, but he was right. The temperature had to have dropped into the forties, and she'd barely worn anything worthy of warding off the chill night air.

Mad Dog reached backward, pulled a sleeping bag over their shoulders and wrapped it around them.

Jolie knew she should resist, but she couldn't. Not when she was shaking so hard and Mad Dog's body was so hot. "How d-did you s-sneak up on m-me s-so easily?" she asked, between chattering teeth.

"I bedded down in the corner of the porch."

"B-but it's so cold out. You could have frozen to death."

"I had the sleeping bag. You can still feel how warm it was. Besides, it's not much warmer in the barn."

She nodded and snuggled closer, absorbing the man's body heat. "Thank you."

His arm tightened around her, but she didn't say anything.

Jolie was glad he didn't. They sat in a long silence. She stared at the stars, not seeing them, but thinking about the man holding her close. How had she come to this? From telling him to leave, to leaning into him as if her life depended on it? She should push him away and send him packing. But she couldn't.

"Missing your father?" Mad Dog asked.

She nodded and wiped the moisture off her cheek. "I

thought I could waltz back in here, get the place in order, catch my terrorist and turn around and sell the ranch. No problem." She snorted. "I was wrong," Jolie whispered. "The place isn't the same as when my father was here."

"Was your father good to you?"

She nodded. "The best father a girl could ever hope to have." She smiled, the tears still ready, but holding off for the moment. "Oh, he didn't do my hair or sew my clothes, but he taught me things I'd need to know as an adult."

"Like?"

"That I can do things myself. I don't need anyone else to build something, fix something or replace parts on an engine. I could do anything I set my mind to."

"Did he teach you to shoot?"

She nodded. "When other girls were getting curling irons and dresses for Christmas, my father got me a rifle. I learned how to shoot using that, and my father's rifle and his shotgun. He taught me how to fire the pistol he carried sometimes to shoot rattlesnakes."

"Sounds like he wanted you to be able to take care of yourself."

Jolie tightened her arms around her legs. "It's like he somehow knew he wouldn't be there for me someday."

"You're lucky," Mad Dog said.

Jolie shot a glance his way, frowning. "Lucky? He was shot while out hunting. He died far too early in his life. He's not here to be there for me when I need someone. He won't walk me down the aisle if I ever get married, which is highly unlikely. After losing him, I can't see investing my heart in anyone else. Why bother, when they could up and die on me?" She sighed. "He'll never know grandchildren, and if I do have a kid someday, my kid will never know what a great man his grandfather was."

As she'd talked, Mad Dog stiffened against her. "You're lucky you had a good father for as long as you did. You're lucky your memories are happy. No one can take those away from you. You're lucky he cared enough to teach you anything." Mad Dog's voice wasn't necessarily harsh, but it was tightly controlled and distant.

She sighed. "You're right. I need to think about what I had, not about what I lost. Most women never have the kind of close relationship I had with my father. If not for him, I wouldn't be the person I am today." For a long moment, she sat in silence, letting the good memories flow over her. Riding horseback alongside her father, mending fences, worming cattle, lying out on a hill under the stars, talking about the constellations or saying nothing at all. "What about you, Caleb? What was your family like?"

"Not like yours," he said, his words clipped, his tone stony.

She gave him a moment or two of silence, but her curiosity got the better of her. She wanted to know more about this man who'd come to be her partner for this mission. "You know where I grew up," she said softly. "Where did you grow up?"

"Houston."

"Do you have brothers and sisters?" she asked.

"No." He shifted, his arm loosening around her.

"Like me. An only child."

He shook his head. "Nothing like you. Your father gave a damn about you."

"And yours didn't?"

"He only cared how about fast I could bring him his next beer." Mad Dog's words came out between tight lips. "Although, I have to say, he taught me a few important life lessons."

"What were they?"

"Don't rely on anyone else for your own food and shelter. Be prepared to work for it."

Holy hell. Had his father not provided for him? She had no words to respond to his revelation.

Mad Dog's voice lowered to little more than a whisper. "And don't give anyone the power to break your heart, because you can't ever rely on the people who are supposed to love you."

As soon as the words left his mouth, Mad Dog wished he hadn't said them. He'd never opened up to anyone about how shitty his life had been growing up. Now, here he was spilling his guts to his new partner. What an idiot. If he wasn't keeping her warm, he'd get up and walk away. She probably thought of him as weak and pathetic.

He waited, cringing inwardly. When she finally spoke, it wasn't what he'd thought she'd say.

She snorted softly. "Okay, well, then we both have commitment issues. It's a good thing we're not falling in love, or we'd be up a crappy creek without life preservers." She pushed the blanket off her shoulders and stood, tugging at the T-shirt to cover as much bare skin as possible. "Since you're already here at the house, and it's getting really cold," she shivered as if to emphasize her point, "you might as well sleep on the couch in the living room."

"You trust me?" he asked rising to his feet.

"I guess I have to. You saved me from a fate worse than death by removing the raccoon from my bedroom. Besides, I sleep with my handgun." Her eyes narrowed. "Try anything, and I'll shoot you."

He raised his hands. "I promise not to try anything…" His lips twisted. "Unless you want me to."

She rolled her eyes. "Don't worry about that. Remember my commitment issues?"

"Sex doesn't have to be about commitment," he reminded her.

"Yeah," she said, her tone flat. "I've learned that in the eight years I've been away. I also learned fraternizing with your partner is never a good idea."

Mad Dog grinned. "Glad to see you're learning to accept it."

She frowned. "Accept what?"

"That we're partners."

She stared at him in the starlight, her eyes narrowing to slits. Finally, she nodded. "Yeah, about that…"

He raised his eyebrows. "Ma'am?"

"I have a terrorist to bring down. You can hang around and pretend to protect me, but don't get in my way, or I'll shoot you to get to him."

Mad Dog pressed a hand to his chest. "Ouch. I see where I rank. But don't worry. I'm here to help, not to hinder."

"Good. Keep thinking like that and we might just get along." A cold breeze lifted the hair off the back of her neck. The illumination from the stars cast her in indigo-blue, softening the contours of her face.

Mad Dog's breath hitched in his chest. Jolie didn't realize just how attractive she was. Any man would be lucky to have her. Lucky that she was strong and competent in her skills. If she entered a relationship, she'd be there as an equal. Not because she needed a man's protection, but because she wanted his love.

Jolie wrapped her jacket around herself and stared up at the stars.

Mad Dog followed her glance to the blanket of twinkling lights filling the heavens. "Something about a clear night sky makes me calm. When my father would come home drunk and yell and break things, I'd leave the trailer and sleep out in the open." His lips stretched into a rueful smile. "I pretended I was an intergalactic traveler, exploring worlds very different from ours. Even when I was at war in the Middle East, the stars seemed to talk to me, to let me know they would always be there."

Jolie's lips turned up on the corners. "My father loved the night sky. I think he would've liked being an astronaut, if he hadn't had this ranch his family left to him."

They stood for another long moment.

Jolie shivered, her body shaking violently.

"You need to get inside before you catch a cold or a bullet from a terrorist."

Jolie didn't argue. She opened the screen door and stepped into the house.

Mad Dog scooped up the sleeping bag and followed.

"Sorry. The couch is all I can offer. I haven't had time to clean any of the other bedrooms." She switched on the light in the living room. "Do you need blankets?"

"No. The sleeping bag will do."

"Good. Because I need to inventory the linens and see if any are worth saving. If one raccoon was in the house, I can imagine mice have been making their homes here as well."

"Again, I'm here to help. No task is too hard or menial."

She chuckled. "Good, the floor needs mopping tomorrow before we head to town."

"Town?"

"I need supplies."

"Shouldn't you be digging in? Watching for Nadir?"

Jolie glanced over her shoulder. "Yes. But I can't just sit and wait."

"That's what I did when I was assigned as a sniper."

"If I were anywhere else, I would do just that. But I'm not. I grew up working this ranch. Sitting around wasn't an option. I have to keep moving or the grief will consume me." She didn't wait for a response, but simply turned and walked down the hallway to her bedroom.

Mad Dog stood rooted to the floor until he heard the sound of her door closing. Then he took the sleeping bag and draped it across the brown leather couch.

The more he thought about Jolie's words, the tighter his chest grew. He'd talked about not loving anyone because of how his parents had treated him. In actuality, he'd learned to care for his teammates and depend on them to have his six.

Then, because he'd been injured, his SEAL family had been taken away from him. His time in the mountains of Colorado had been his time to grieve for his loss and reinforce his belief that investing his heart again would only lead to more pain.

Perhaps, he'd wallowed too long, but now he had purpose. A job to do that had meaning and purpose. The country was under attack by radicalized home-grown terrorists. Jolie was a target because she'd removed one of the terrorists. If he wanted to do the job right, he had to keep his head on straight and not get emotionally involved with his partner.

That should be easy, considering she'd made it clear any advances on his part would be unwanted and shut down in a heartbeat. Or shot down…

Mad Dog chuckled, though he knew he shouldn't. The woman was serious. She'd shoot him if he tried any sexual advances toward her.

His groin tightened like it had while he'd held her in the circle of his arms beneath the sleeping bag. Her curves had pressed against his side, making him more than aware of her as a woman, not just a CIA agent.

That she'd been crying made her even more human and vulnerable, emotionally, if not physically. He was sure she would have taken him down if he'd been the terrorist.

If she'd been fully aware of the danger... He hadn't pointed out her carelessness. At the time, she'd been pretty wrapped in her grief. But had he not been there and Nadir had been lurking in the shadows...Jolie would have been dead.

Setting herself up as a target and luring her predator to her own stomping grounds had been a good idea. But Jolie had some unresolved issues to work through regarding her old home.

Mad Dog hoped she resolved them quickly. If she planned on living through this assignment, she needed to have her head in the game.

Thankfully, he was there to have her back. Lambert had been right to send someone to make sure the terrorist was eliminated. Hopefully, Mad Dog could do that before Nadir had a chance to take out his vengeance on Jolie.

Too wound up to lie down, Mad Dog did another search of the house to make sure the windows and doors remained locked. He paused in front of Jolie's bedroom door, imagining her with her hand beneath her pillow, resting on her pistol. No way he'd open that door, unless she invited him in. And he'd only enter on the condition she set the gun aside.

His lips curled. Would he take her up on an invitation to join her in her bedroom for other than raccoon removal?

Oh, hell, yeah. The woman was built for making love

—strong, powerful and with curves in all the right places.

Mad Dog switched off the light in the living room and lay on his back on the couch, staring up at the ceiling, illuminated by the starlight peeking through the window.

Yesterday, he'd been alone on a mountain, contemplating throwing himself off a cliff. Today, he was very glad he hadn't.

Despite her arguments to the contrary, Jolie needed him. He hoped, with his bum leg and all, that he he'd be able to help when the time came.

CHAPTER 6

THE RAPID REPORT of gunfire jerked Mad Dog awake. He blinked his eyes open, wondering if he'd been dreaming.

Sunlight streamed through the curtains into the living room. After lying awake for most of the night, he must have fallen asleep in the wee hours of the morning.

Had he been asleep, reliving the last firefight in that village in Afghanistan? Or had he really heard gunfire?

Mad Dog sat up, dragged on his boots and leaped to his feet. His heart racing, he ran down the hallway to Jolie's bedroom. The door stood open, the room empty and the bed made.

Bang! Bang! Bang!

This time he was wide-awake and the sound was definitely that of gunfire. He hurried through the kitchen and out the back door into the chilly morning air.

His first instinct was to survey the area, searching

for bad guys. He scanned the bushes, shadows and corners of the barn. As far as he could tell, no one stood by ready to take out the woman alone in the barnyard.

Jolie stood in the morning sunshine, wearing jeans, cowboy boots and a dark bomber jacket and facing one of the pasture fences. Her strawberry-blond hair was pulled back into a ponytail at the base of her neck, and she wore no makeup, the freckles across her nose standing out in sharp contrast to her pale skin. She held a pistol in her right hand with her left hand braced beneath it.

On a fence rail several yards away stood a line of five soda cans.

Jolie stood steady, her arms parallel to the ground and fired.

For each shot, a can jumped into the air and fell to the ground.

When she'd finished, she slid back the bolt on her weapon, checked for any unexpended rounds and allowed the bolt to ride forward when she'd determined it was empty. Then she glanced toward the house.

Mad Dog descended the steps off the back porch and crossed the yard toward her.

"Sorry, did I wake you?" she asked, her lip turned up in a smirk.

"I should have been awake already." Mad Dog ran a hand through his hair. "Do you always start your day with target practice?"

"Only when I'm here on the ranch, and I can't sleep." Her lips twisted. "Care to give it a shot?" She handed him her pistol and a box of bullets from her jacket pocket. "While you reload, I'll set up the cans."

He took the offering, dropped the magazine into his palm and loaded it. "Is this some kind of test?"

"Maybe," she said without turning around. One by one, she set up six empty soda cans. When she was done, she rejoined him. "Why? Are you too sleepy to handle it?"

The sound of gunfire had jerked him from dead sleep to fully awake. "I can handle it," he said. Though he preferred to use weapons he was familiar with, he was confident he could manage at close range.

He aimed the handgun at the soda can, breathed in and out then caressed the trigger.

The can flew into the air.

"Lucky shot," Jolie commented beside him. "Can you do it again?"

Ignoring her taunt, he aimed and fired again, hitting the second can, sending it flying into the air.

"Not bad for a rusty SEAL," she said.

He squeezed off three more rounds, hitting all three cans.

On the final shot, he aimed carefully.

"Can you do it, while distracted?" she asked.

He ignored her question, the cold air raising goose-flesh on his arms, and concentrated on hitting the can. Slowly, he squeezed his finger on the trigger.

At the same time, Jolie leaned closer and blew a stream of warm air at his neck.

Mad Dog's hand jerked and the shot went wide of the can.

Jolie's laughter echoed off the nearby hillsides. "Sorry, I couldn't resist." She chuckled. "You should see your face."

"That was a dangerous thing to do," he said, frowning.

She nodded. "You're right. You might've shot me. My apologies." Jolie held out her hand. "My weapon?"

He dropped the magazine out of the pistol, pulled back the bolt and set the safety before handing it back to her.

She arched an eyebrow. "Afraid I'll shoot you?"

"You keep promising you'll shoot me. Why shouldn't I believe you?"

"I said I'd shoot you, *if* you tried anything funny." She reloaded the magazine, checked that the safety was set and slipped the weapon into the shoulder holster beneath her jacket. When she glanced up, the early morning sun glinted off her bright green eyes. The woman didn't look anything like what Mad Dog would have thought a CIA agent should.

"I thought we'd head on into town, have breakfast at the diner and then hit the hardware store," Jolie said.

Mad Dog nodded, tempted to reach out and touch her face to see if her skin was as soft as it appeared. His hand was halfway up when he realized what he was doing. He dropped it to his side. "I'm ready when you are. Let me grab my jacket. If we're getting supplies, we can take my truck."

She smiled. "Good, because I want to pick up some T-posts and barbed wire, and I'm not sure the posts will fit in the back of my SUV."

Mad Dog gave an exaggerated sigh. "Finally, I'm good for something." He started toward the house. "Are you coming?"

"Right behind you."

He snorted. "I'd prefer you walked ahead of me and save your target practice for when I'm awake."

"Again, I'm used to working alone. It didn't occur to me to ask your permission to step outside."

He shook his head. "Humor me, will ya?"

She stared at him for a long moment, her eyes narrowed. Then she nodded. "Fair enough. I understand you can't perform your assignment if I don't cooperate. As long as your work doesn't interfere with mine, I'll try to remember to include you."

His lips twitched. "That's all I ask."

She stepped in front of him and entered the house first.

Moments later, Mad Dog shrugged into his jacket and led the way out the front door, checking all directions for movement.

When he was certain no threat existed, he held the door for Jolie.

"Remind me not to get used to someone opening doors for me," she said as she exited.

Though his father had never opened a door for any woman, Mad Dog had learned the value of the kindness from visiting Mrs. Beggs, the old lady who'd lived in the same trailer park where he'd grown up. Though she had little money, she had taken great pride in her appearance and encouraged Mad Dog to take pride in his.

She'd taught him the manners his father was sorely lacking.

When he'd been younger, he'd hide out at her trailer while his father cursed and threw things in a drunken fit. Eventually, her sons had moved her into a nursing home, and she hadn't been there when he needed a place to go.

Mrs. Beggs would have been proud of him opening doors for women. Even if the woman was a CIA agent, fully capable of opening her own door. The old lady had said it wasn't that women weren't able to, but that by opening the door, men proved their respect.

Mad Dog hurried around Jolie to open the truck door for her.

She gave him a narrow-eyed glance but didn't say a word as she climbed into the cab.

He spent the drive into town studying the road, the turn-offs and the other vehicles coming and going.

Once in the little town of Eagle Rock he made a mental list of the businesses, glad to see there was a tavern. When they caught their man, he'd celebrate with a beer. In the meantime, he refused to consume alcohol, knowing it would dull his wits. In order to keep Jolie safe, he'd need a clear head at all times.

The diner was on one end of Main Street.

"I would have made breakfast this morning," Jolie said. "But the cook at the diner does a better job and has bacon. I picked up eggs, but no bacon."

"I don't expect you to cook for me. I can manage on my own." Mad Dog stated. "and you're right. Breakfast isn't complete without bacon."

"My thoughts exactly." She grinned. "The diner and the tavern are also great places to get all the gossip. If anyone new shows up in town, you'll hear it first at one of those two places."

Mad Dog pulled into the diner parking lot and backed into a parking space. If they needed to leave quickly, they wouldn't have to take the time to back out.

Jolie led the way inside. A bell over the door jingled as they entered.

A waitress called out, "Seat yourself anywhere you like. I'll be with you in a minute."

Jolie smiled at the woman, chose a seat in a booth and sat with her back to the wall.

"Mind if I sit beside you?" Mad Dog asked.

She gave him a twisted grin. "Let me guess. You like to sit with your back to the wall as well?"

He nodded. "It comes with the job."

"Right." She scooted over and let him slide in next to her.

When his thigh touched hers, a blast of electricity bolted through his veins. He pulled back a little, leaving a gap between them. Unfortunately, every time one of them moved, they bumped again.

Perhaps he'd be better off sitting across the table from her. However, he remained where he was, knowing it was the right thing to do. With his back to the door and windows, he wouldn't see who entered or stood outside the diner, aiming a weapon at Jolie.

The bell jingled, announcing another guest entering the building.

The man wore a dark brown uniform with a shiny

badge. He was tall, with sandy-blond hair and a ready smile. When he turned toward Mad Dog and Jolie, his smile grew wider, and he headed straight for them.

"Jolie? Jolie Richards? Is that really you?" The man stopped at their table.

"Chase?" Jolie laughed. "What the hell? Since when did you start wearing a deputy sheriff's uniform?"

Mad Dog slid out of the booth, allowing Jolie to rise and throw her arms around the deputy's neck and hug him.

Mad Dog stood back, his fists clenching. Why it bothered him that she showed affection for another man, he didn't know. But it did. He wanted to yank her back and stand between the two.

He had to talk himself down, rationalizing that she wasn't his girlfriend, wife or fiancée. He had no right to be jealous when he'd only met the woman the day before.

Jolie stepped back and waved a hand toward Mad Dog. "Chase Wells, this is…"

Mad Dog stuck out his hand. "Caleb Maddox, Jolie's fiancé."

Chase's eyebrows rose up into the hair falling down over his forehead. "Fiancé?" He grabbed Mad Dog's hand and gave it a firm shake. "You're one lucky man. Jolie was my best friend in high school. She wasn't like all the other girls. She liked to hunt, fish, hike and ride horses. There wasn't anything she couldn't do as well as any man or better."

Jolie's lips twisted into a smiling frown. "You make me sound like one of the guys."

Chase laughed. "No way. You were way prettier to look at than the guys."

"She is pretty amazing," Mad Dog said. "I couldn't pass all of that up." He slipped an arm around Jolie's waist, perfectly prepared for her to knee him in the groin for the effort.

But she didn't. Instead, she motioned toward the empty seat across the table. "Would you like to join us?"

"I don't want to horn in on you two lovebirds."

"You're not horning in." Jolie leaned into Mad Dog and squeezed his arm. "I'd love to catch up on what's going on around here."

"If you're sure...?" Chase glanced from Jolie to Mad Dog.

Mad Dog nodded. "Please. Join us."

"Okay, then. I haven't had breakfast, and they make the best waffles in the county." Chase waited for Jolie to sit before he slid into the seat across from her.

The pretty blond waitress stopped at the table and smiled at the deputy first. "Hi, Deputy Wells." Then she turned her bright smile on Jolie and Mad Dog. "I'm Daisy. I'll be your server. What can I get you?"

"Coffee," all three people at the table said at once.

Daisy laughed. "I'll be right back with the coffee and to take your order." She flounced away.

Deputy Wells leaned his elbows on the table and stared across at Jolie. "I can't believe you're back after all these years."

"The last I heard, you were on the rodeo circuit, riding bulls." Jolie nodded at his uniform. "When did this happen?"

The deputy shrugged. "A couple years ago I had a pretty bad fall. The bull gored me in the ribs and punctured a lung. I was laid up with a few broken bones and difficulty breathing. I couldn't see myself doing that again. So, here I am, one of Eagle Rock's finest." He winked.

Mad Dog took it all in, wondering what it felt like to come back to a place where you liked the people you grew up with. He couldn't imagine going back to the trailer park in Houston. For one, the turnover would have been complete. He wouldn't know anyone there now. Hell, the park might have been bulldozed to make room for a parking lot or something.

The kids he knew in school had likely gone to jail or were killed in drive-by shootings. They hadn't gone on to become sheriff's deputies or pillars of the community.

"Are you happy?" Jolie asked.

Deputy Wells nodded. "Sometimes, I miss the excitement of the rodeo circuit. But I don't miss the abuse on my body. And we get our own excitement around here."

She raised her eyebrows. "Oh, yeah? I don't remember it being very exciting in Eagle Rock."

"Well, we've had some of our local celebrities attacked by stalkers or rapists."

"That's not reassuring for the residents," Mad Dog murmured.

The deputy nodded. "Thankfully, the people responsible have been captured or killed."

Jolie shook her head. "It's not the same as when we grew up."

"It hasn't been the same since your father was killed. I've opened the case file and looked over the evidence," Deputy Wells said. "I even went so far as to question some of the people in town, asking if anyone had a problem with your father." The man shook his head, a slight smile curling his lips. "No one had a bad thing to say about your dad. He was awesome."

Jolie's lips pressed into a thin line. "I can understand someone having a hunting accident. But why wouldn't that person come forward and admit it? Or, at the very least, help the man he shot?"

Deputy Wells reached across the table and placed his hand over hers. "I don't know why people do the things they do. Just when I think I've seen it all, something else happens."

"Well, I hope things have settled down in Eagle Rock," Mad Dog said.

"I wish they had." The deputy glanced at him and back to Jolie. "But they haven't."

Jolie pulled her hand out from under the deputy's and leaned back. "What's happening now?"

"I don't know if you realize, but the town is changing. Folks from California are buying up the land and ranches, driving prices up. Our local young people are finding it hard to get jobs that will pay them enough so they can afford to buy their own homes. Some can't find jobs, period."

"I thought most young people moved to bigger cities to work." Jolie said.

"Most. But some of those who remain are angry and

resentful of the rich people coming in and buying up all the old ranches."

"How do you know they're angry?" Mad Dog asked. "Are they telling you this?"

The deputy's jaw tightened. "They're acting out. We don't have proof, but we think they've formed some kind of gang. We also think part of the initiation into the gang is to perform some sort of rite of passage."

"For example?" Jolie prompted.

"The old, abandoned railroad depot burned to the ground last weekend."

Jolie frowned. "You think young people did it?"

Deputy Wells nodded. "The fire chief said it was arson, started with an accelerant like gasoline. Again, we don't have evidence, so we can't arrest anyone. But we're still investigating."

Mad Dog crossed his arms over his chest. "No one saw anything?"

"The railroad depot was on the outside edge of town. The closest person to the depot was old Mrs. Rheinhardt. She's deaf in both ears and goes to bed around eight o'clock every night. Dispatch got the call around two in the morning when someone leaving the Blue Moose Tavern spotted the flames."

"What makes you think this gang is responsible?" Mad Dog asked.

"The spray paint on the brick. It's the same graffiti we found during another incident involving the destruction of a deputy sheriff's patrol vehicle."

Jolie gasped. "They were that brazen they'd attack a patrol car?"

"Yeah. Here, look." He pulled out his cell phone and touched the screen until a photo appeared of a sheriff's vehicle painted with a bright red swastika.

"The vehicle was parked in front of one of the deputy's houses. Again, on the edge of town. He made a habit of stopping for dinner with his wife. While he was eating, someone tagged his vehicle with spray paint."

"In Eagle Rock?" Jolie shook her head. "This town is small enough everyone knows everyone else's business. How are they getting away with it?"

"We suspect they have a secret meeting location in the hills." The deputy's eyes narrowed. "For that matter, keep your eyes open. Your place has been more or less abandoned for eight years. They could be in one of the caves we used to play in when we were kids."

"Wow. This isn't the same place I remember," Jolie said.

"It's still a good town with good people. It's just that some are having a harder time keeping up with the changes than others."

Daisy returned with the coffee and set three steaming mugs in front of them. "I couldn't help overhearing your conversation," she said. "I'm betting I grew up with some of those young people who are causing all the trouble."

Deputy Wells turned to her, his brows descending. "Can you name the members of the gang?"

She pressed a hand to her chest. "No, but I can name the people my age who stuck around Eagle Rock."

"Like?"

"Steve Neilson, Dalton Talbert, Alec Jenner, Brandon

Lewis, Colleen Porter, Kylie Laster, and Marcus Sweeney, to name a few." She held up her hands. "But I'm not saying any of them are members of a gang." She glanced over her shoulder, her smile fading. "I have too much on my own plate to hang out with gangs, so I stay out of it."

"You're smart to stay out of it," the deputy said. "It could only cause you trouble."

"I've got enough of that taking care of my father and helping out with the little bit of farming he does." She smiled. "It's a shame so many of the kids my age left town. And the ones who stayed have changed from when they were back in school."

"Who has changed?" Jolie asked.

Daisy rolled her eyes toward the ceiling. "Well, Colleen got married straight out of school and divorced a year later. She's a little down on men and life in general. I can't blame her. She works at the tavern when she's not scrubbing floors for the real estate agent." Daisy tapped her chin. "Brandon Lewis and I used to be sweet on each other back when we were in middle school. Then one day he just quit coming over and talking to me. He still shies away from me when we see each other in passing. And Marcus Sweeney is a jerk. But then he's always been a jerk." Daisy pulled out her pad and pencil from her pocket. "But I've talked long enough. Are you ready to order?"

Jolie ordered eggs, bacon and toast. Mad Dog ordered the same, adding an order of hash brown potatoes. The deputy ordered waffles and bacon.

Once Daisy left the table, Mad Dog sipped on his

coffee, digesting everything Deputy Wells and Daisy had said. "Have you had any new people come to town who could have stirred up the gang?" Mad Dog asked.

The deputy's eyes narrowed. "We've had some pipeline workers staying above the tavern, but they're on the road early in the morning and don't get back until late in the evening. They spend most of their time in the tavern after work, eating dinner and drinking beer." Wells shook his head. "No, they seem relatively harmless, hardworking and oblivious to town politics."

"Anyone else?"

He shook his head. "We have had a few former military folks new to these parts. They're working for Hank Patterson's security group, the Brotherhood Protectors. But they're a great bunch of vets. Hank's done good things with them."

Mad Dog nodded. Hank saved his ass when he might have thrown himself over a cliff. The man had a heart and an idea of what his fellow warriors needed to survive.

Purpose.

"If you notice anyone new in town, will you let me know?" Jolie asked.

Deputy Wells nodded. "Sure. But why?"

She looked toward Mad Dog. "I might have a stalker."

Deputy Wells ran a hand through his hair. "He wouldn't be the first here in Eagle Rock. Hank's wife, Sadie, had one."

"Why would Hank's wife have a stalker?" Jolie asked.

The deputy's eyes widened. "You didn't know?"

Jolie shook her head. "I haven't kept in touch very well."

"She's Sadie McClain. The Hollywood megastar actress lives right here in Eagle Rock."

"Oh," Jolie nodded. "*That* Sadie."

Mad Dog had heard of her, too. Who hadn't? "Hank's married to Sadie McClain?"

Jolie shook her head. "Wow. I didn't realize he'd married Sadie. Those two were tight in high school. But they split up after graduating."

"Actually, Sadie is the reason Hank got the idea for the Brotherhood Protectors. She came home because she'd had problems with a stalker. The stalker followed her here, and she needed a bodyguard to protect her from her stalker. She hasn't been the only one. With the influx of all the rich folks, they have their own issues and need protection."

"Sounds like Hank has his work cut out for him," Mad Dog said. "Did they catch Sadie's stalker?"

"Yes, they did. And that's when Hank caught Sadie and made her his wife." Deputy Wells grinned. "They have a baby girl, now. Hank's never been happier."

Daisy returned a few minutes later with their plates laid out on her arms. She set them down one by one and stood back. "Can I get anything else? Catsup for your hash browns? Jelly, more coffee?"

"No, thank you," Jolie said.

Mad Dog inhaled the scent of fresh, fried bacon. After fending for himself on a camp stove for the last few months, it was nice to let someone else do the cooking. He tucked into the meal, not uttering another word until his plate was clean of every speck of eggs, hash browns and toast.

"You want some of mine?" Jolie shoved her half-eaten plate of food his direction. "You act like you haven't eaten in a month."

She had no idea how close to the truth she was. Other than eating the contents of some of the canned goods and dried beans left behind by Kujo, Mad Dog had hunted for rabbit and squirrel to provide protein in his diet. Bacon didn't keep for long without refrigeration. Since the cabin had been without electricity, he'd had to hunt for his food, or drive down the mountain into a nearby town for supplies or go hungry.

Many days, he'd gone hungry.

But not today. Today was a breakfast feast.

As Deputy Wells was drinking the last sips of his coffee, the radio on his shoulder squawked. "That's my cue." He threw down a napkin and enough money to cover his portion of the bill and slipped out of the booth. "Good to see you, Jolie." He held out his hand to her. "Don't get up. Duty calls, but you might as well enjoy the rest of your meal."

"It's good to see you again, Chase," Jolie said.

"And you. Nice to meet you, Caleb." He touched his fingertips to his temple in a mock salute. "I'll see you around."

Jolie smiled. "You bet."

After the man left, Jolie pushed her unfinished plate away. "I didn't know things were so bad here."

"Seems like it's always a very few people who make an entire community miserable." The gangs in his neighborhood terrorized the good people as well as the bad. Drive-by shooters didn't always make other gang members the victims.

Jolie snorted. "And I thought I'd have it easy identifying a single terrorist in a small town in the middle of nowhere, Montana."

"You don't know you'll have problems with the local gang."

"No, but I need to know if they're on my ranch. And if they are, I need to get them off. I don't want to be caught in the crossfire of gang warfare and an ISIS terrorist."

"Fair enough," Mad Dog said. "Let's get those errands run and get back out to the ranch. Hopefully, we'll see someone coming from far enough away we can get a bead on them and take them out, before they have a chance to get to you."

Jolie tossed her napkin on the table and waited for Mad Dog to scoot out of the booth.

Once he stood, he held out his hand to assist her to her feet.

Her foot must have caught on the table leg, because she pitched into Mad Dog.

Still holding her hand, he pulled her against him and wrapped his arm around her waist. With Jolie pressed against him, every nerve in his body lit up like the Fourth of July.

"Sorry," she said and pressed her hands to his chest. When she glanced up into his face, her cheeks were flushed and her eyes a deeper shade of green. Her tongue swept across her pale, pink lips, and her gaze dropped to his. For a moment, her fingers curled into his shirt.

Then she pushed away and stood on her own, a few steps away from him.

If Mad Dog wasn't mistaken, Jolie had felt whatever electric jolt had gone off between them.

Yeah, this assignment might just get a whole lot harder.

CHAPTER 7

JOLIE COULDN'T GET out of the diner fast enough. What in the hell had just happened? She'd tripped. No big deal. The big deal had come when she'd landed in Mad Dog's arms. And liked it!

She didn't need to fall for the man. She had a job to do, and he wasn't part of it.

Mad Dog drove the two blocks to the Bartlett's Hardware and parked.

"I'll only be a few minutes if you want to wait here." Jolie didn't wait for a response, jumped down from the truck and hurried into the store.

Mad Dog wasn't far behind her.

She had hoped he'd stay in the truck and give her a few minutes to get her act together. Her body's reaction to the man was unprecedented. She'd never had such a strong physical reaction to any man. Until Mad Dog.

Fortunately, he gave her a little space by wandering

down different aisles. But she could feel his gaze on her at all times.

"Can I help you?" A young man wearing a light blue T-shirt with the Bartlett Hardware logo stopped in front of Jolie.

"I need barbed wire, fence staples and T-posts." She handed him the list she'd written that morning.

The young man hurried to gather the items on her list and carried them out to the truck.

All the while, Mad Dog followed her, close enough to be there in a flash and far enough away she couldn't hit him.

Jolie felt protected and irritated all at the same time. By the time they were in the truck and on their way, she was ready to scream. "I think I could have handled the hardware store by myself," she said. "I'm not used to having someone hover around me like a mother hen."

"Sorry, to crowd you, but you never know when someone will walk up to you all friendly-like and run a knife into your ribs." He pulled out of the parking lot and paused. "Which way?"

"To the Lewis's ranch. Tom promised to loan me a couple of horses while I'm here."

"Yeah, I meant to ask you, why two?"

She stared across the seat toward him. "I assume you'll go where I go." She narrowed her eyes. "You do know how to ride, don't you?"

"How hard can it be? Like riding a motorcycle with legs, right?"

Jolie clapped a hand to her forehead. "What were they thinking sending a city boy out to a ranch?"

"I'm sure I'll catch on quickly."

"I hope so. The four-wheelers in the barn have been sitting for eight years. They probably need a complete overhaul before they'll work. So, unless you can perform miracles on old machinery, you'll be learning how to ride."

"How do you plan on getting the horses over to the ranch?" he asked.

"I'd planned on riding them home."

"You can't ride two, and you're not going alone."

Jolie bit down hard on her tongue. As much as she'd like the time by herself, she'd be a fool to ride out without her backup. If she was killed while trying to prove a point, Nadir would get away to kill again.

She sighed. "While I'm borrowing horses, I'll ask Tom if we can use his horse trailer."

Mad Dog nodded, apparently satisfied with her answer.

Twenty minutes later, they arrived in front of the Lewis ranch house. Jolie dropped down from the truck and started toward the house.

Sherry stepped out on the porch, wiping her hands on a dishtowel. "Hi Jolie, Caleb." She tipped her head to the side. "Tom is expecting you. You can find him out by the barn."

Mad Dog joined Jolie. Together, they walked around the house toward the barn.

Tom emerged from a paddock, leading a palomino mare. He glanced toward them and smiled. "There you are. I was wondering when you'd stop by."

"I wanted to get to the hardware store for supplies. I'm sure I'll have some fences needing some attention."

"They shouldn't be too bad." Tom led the palomino into the barn. "I kept up with them over the years, but the last time I was out, was a couple months ago."

Jolie followed, admiring the mare. "Is this one of the horses you're going to loan me?"

"If you want her," Tom said. "She's a little spirited, but nothing you can't handle."

"I'll need a really gentle horse for Caleb," she said, wrinkling her nose. "He's new to ranch life."

Tom grinned at Mad Dog over the back of the palomino. "I have just the mount for you. Topper is a little older, but he's as gentle as they come. I'd put my gray-haired grandmother on him without a worry."

Mad Dog chuckled. "Nice to know I'm being compared to a grandmother. But thanks."

"Tom," Jolie said, "do you have a horse trailer I can transport them back to my place with?"

"Sure. Is your truck equipped with a drag hitch?"

Mad Dog nodded. "It is."

"You can use my two-horse trailer."

"Do you need it back right away?"

"No. Keep it to bring the horses back when you don't need them anymore." He ran a brush over the mare's back. "Now, what about tack?"

"I need everything," Jolie said.

"Brandon!" Tom yelled. When no one answered, the rancher shook his head. "He was here a minute ago. I don't know where he disappears to. But never mind. I can get you fixed up."

An hour later, they had two horses loaded into the back of the trailer. They loaded saddles, bridles, blankets, feed and hay, necessary for a couple of days, in the bed of Mad Dog's truck.

"Hopefully, we won't need them more than a week. And I'll replenish your feed and hay at that time, unless you need it sooner," Jolie said.

Tom waved her offer away. "Don't worry about it. I'm hoping you'll decide to stay. I like knowing I have neighbor watching over the place. There's been too many strange things happening around the county lately."

"Like what?" Jolie asked, though she'd already heard from Chase about the gang-related activity.

"I don't know. I was out a couple nights ago and thought I heard the roar of small engines, like at a motorcycle race."

"Coming from which direction?" Mad Dog asked.

"I couldn't be certain. Sound echoes off the hills around here. It could have been from your place or on the opposite side of my spread." Tom shrugged. "You know how it is." He locked gazes with Jolie.

"Yeah. It's frustrating when you can hear the bawl of a cow, but can't tell from which direction it's coming." She smiled. "My father and I spent many hours riding over pastures in the complete wrong direction."

"I hope whoever was out riding after midnight wasn't doing so on your property." Tom laid a hand on Jolie's shoulder. "And if they were, that they won't do it again. You take care of yourself. For what it's worth, I'm glad you're home."

"Thanks for everything, Tom." Jolie glanced at Mad Dog. "Are you okay driving with a trailer?"

Mad Dog nodded. "I might not have ridden a horse, but I have driven a truck, towing a trailer." He settled in behind the wheel and circled the barnyard, heading out the way they'd come into the Lewis's ranch.

As they pulled around in the barnyard, Mad Dog saw a young man with brown hair and brown eyes standing in the shadows, watching them. He looked again, and the boy was gone. Perhaps he's imagined it. Why would Tom's son hide from them? Or was he only hiding from work? Mad Dog shook it off. It didn't matter. They'd gotten what they needed and were headed back to the Rocking R Ranch.

Jolie sat in her seat, staring out the front window, scanning the woods around them. "What's wrong with the world? Have people lost their minds?"

"Sounds like this area has had its share of troubles."

"No kidding. I hope whatever it is doesn't get tangled up with Nadir's kind of crazy."

Mad Dog reached out and took her hand in his. "Hey, it'll be all right. Whatever happens, I've got your back."

She gave his fingers a squeeze, and held on. "Thanks. I guess I'm glad you showed up when you did."

"You guess?" Mad Dog chuckled. "Thanks for your vote of confidence. But seriously, I'm here for you. We'll face whatever comes our way together."

Jolie held onto Mad Dog's hand. The strength and comfort she got out of that simple gesture filled her heart and made her chest swell.

He might be overprotective and far too attractive, but he was good to have around. The man had skills, or he wouldn't have made it as a SEAL. He'd be an asset to her mission and to keeping her alive until they found and dealt with Nadir. They had to stop his brand of terrorism before anyone else got hurt. The job wasn't the problem. Waiting was.

MAD DOG PULLED through the gate at the Rocking R Ranch, taking it slow over the cattle guard, trying not to disturb the horses in the trailer behind them.

He'd towed equipment and the occasional trailer full of all his worldly goods, but he'd never transported live cargo.

"You don't have to go so slow. The horses are used to being transported in a trailer."

The gravel road leading through the trees to the ranch house had seen better days and needed to be graded and smoothed. "If it's okay with you, I'd prefer to go slow."

She sat back and smiled. "I would like to take the horses out before it gets dark and check things out for myself."

"Point taken." He glanced up at a bright, sunny sky. "It's not even noon yet. You'll have time."

"True." Jolie rolled down the window and leaned her head out. The wind whipped her strawberry-blond hair out of the ponytail and flung it around her face.

She looked like a teenager on her way to summer

camp, not a seasoned CIA agent, waiting to kill a terrorist.

Suddenly she sat up straighter. "Do you hear that?"

Mad Dog hit the button to lower his window and slowed the vehicle to a stop. Without the crunch of gravel beneath the tires, he could hear the whine of engines, growing louder, as if heading their way.

"Think we're going to get up close and personal with the people Tom heard out riding at midnight."

Mad Dog pressed his foot to the accelerator and eased forward, aware of the horses in the trailer behind him, but determined to find out what was going on ahead of them.

When they came out of the trees into the open, Jolie gasped. "My house!"

Half a dozen dirt bikes and four-wheelers circled the ranch house, stirring up dust. Someone had spray-painted red graffiti all over the exterior walls and windows of the ranch house.

When one of the riders spotted the truck, he turned and headed straight for them. He wore a dark helmet, dark jeans and a black leather jacket. The rest of the gang was similarly dressed. Once the leader turned away from the house, the others followed suit, flying over the ground, hell-bent on raising a ruckus.

Mad Dog shifted the truck into park. "No matter what happens, stay in the truck," he said.

"Like hell, I will." Jolie started to open her door.

Mad Dog reached across and grabbed her arm. "You're who Nadir is coming for. If something happens to you, he'll disappear. He won't come looking for me. He'll get away. You have to stay safe until we get him."

He'd voiced what Jolie had thought all along. She let go of the door handle and stared across at him. "What are you going to do?"

"Catch me one of these bastards and find out what the hell's going on." He waited until the first rider was close, then flung open his door, dove out and lunged for the man. He grabbed the guy's sleeve, but couldn't hold on.

The man swerved, right then left and fell over. He was up and back on the bike before Mad Dog could get to him again.

The others saw what had happened and raced toward Mad Dog.

One pulled out a handgun.

As the shot rang out, Mad Dog tucked and rolled to the right, springing to his feet. He grabbed a stick from the ground and went after the next guy, swinging hard.

He hit the biker in the chest and knocked him off his bike.

The man landed on his back and lay still for a moment.

Mad Dog started for him, but didn't get two feet before he was cut off by a biker nearly running him over.

He jumped back to avoid being hit. After the guy passed, Mad Dog started again for the man lying on the ground, just beginning to stir.

Another biker came close to running him over.

Mad Dog threw himself to the side and rolled over,

pulling the handgun from his shoulder holster beneath his jacket.

The dude with the gun came at him.

Mad Dog knelt and aimed.

A moment before he pulled the trigger, a shot rang out, and the man on the bike dropped to the ground. His bike continued forward.

Mad Dog rolled to the left, narrowly avoiding the front tire. He glanced toward the truck.

Jolie stood in the door, resting her hands on the roof of the truck, her pistol pointing at Mad Dog.

Mad Dog ducked.

A shot rang out.

He could almost feel the whoosh of the bullet as it skimmed over the top of his head and hit something behind him.

He turned to see a biker swerve away from him.

The guy he'd knocked off his bike was on his feet, running toward his ride. He pulled it up from the ground, jammed his foot on the starter and gave the throttle a twist. And then he was gone.

The lead guy had circled back and stopped beside the guy Jolie had tagged. The man held his arm close to his side, but managed to get up onto the back of the leader's bike.

Mad Dog ran after them, cursing his limp. He wasn't quite fast enough to catch up.

"Caleb! Look out!"

A glance over his shoulder made Mad Dog change directions. He jagged to his right as a biker raced up behind him. The biker swung out a booted foot and kicked Mad Dog in his bad leg.

Mad Dog went down, pain shooting through his leg and all the way up into his back.

"Fuck!" Ignoring the knifing pain, he knelt in the dirt and aimed his weapon at the retreating figures. But it was too late. He'd missed his opportunity to catch one of the jerks.

He remained poised to shoot for a few seconds longer, in case the gang returned for more of the same. When they sound of the motorcycle engines faded into the distance, Mad Dog rose to his feet and limped back to the truck.

Jolie had left the cab and walked to the back of the trailer. She was speaking softly to the horses.

They pawed and whickered, their eyes rolling back in their heads.

She talked softly, soothing them with nonsensical words. Just the sound of her voice calmed them and, soon, they were standing still.

All in all, Mad Dog could have kicked himself. He'd failed completely. If not for Jolie, he'd have been injured, if not killed. Then she'd have been left to defend herself. "Thanks," he said, grudgingly. He was angrier with himself than anything.

Jolie walked around the back of the trailer and laid a hand on his shoulder. "Are you all right?"

He shrugged off her hand and nodded. "I'm fine. Stupid, but fine."

"How do you figure?"

"A man with a limp, catching a man on a motorcycle?" He snorted. "What was I thinking?"

She cupped his cheek with her palm. "I thought it was pretty amazing. You almost had the first guy, and the way you hit the other one with the stick was inspirational." She leaned up on her toes. "Impressive." And she kissed him full on the lips.

Mad Dog stood still. Stunned. His leg hurt, and he was still mad at himself, but the kiss had knocked his mental self-flagellation on its ass.

He cupped his hand to the back of hers still resting on his cheek. "Why did you do that?"

She raised and lowered her shoulders. "I don't know. But, please, don't make a big deal out of it. We need to get the horses out of the trailer and check out the damage to the house."

He pulled her hand off his face and pressed his lips to her palm. "Thanks again for saving my sorry ass."

"Yeah? Well, I expect you to stick around and save mine in return." She winked and slipped free of his grip. "Drive, Caleb. We have work to do."

Mad Dog pulled his sore ass up into the truck and drove to the barn. "We need to notify the sheriff about this incident. They could be checking local hospitals for anyone coming in with a gunshot wound."

"We will, but later," she assured him. "We need to get the horses out of the trailer and make sure they weren't injured in the excitement."

They unloaded the horses from the trailer and led them into stalls.

"I'll unload the rest," Mad Dog offered.

"It will take less time if we do it together," she said, lifting a saddle out of the truck bed.

Mad Dog took the other and followed her into the barn and tack room where they laid the saddles on the dusty saddletrees.

"My father used to keep this place spotless. He kept the saddles in the best working order." She ran her hands over a set of punches used to poke holes in leather. "It's like walking through a haunted house. I see him everywhere, and yet, he's gone and most of the things he loved are gone."

The sorrow in her voice hit Mad Dog square in the chest, making it hurt worse than his bum leg. He turned her around and pulled her into his arms. "He's still here."

Jolie looked up into his eyes, her own swimming in unshed tears. "How do you figure?" She swallowed hard and looked down.

"He still lives in your heart." He touched her chin, guiding it upward. "You have good memories of him. Be glad you have those. No one can take those away. They can't be stolen, sold or auctioned off. They're yours forever."

Then despite his better judgment, he bent and pressed his lips to hers.

CHAPTER 8

Jolie forgot to breathe.

The first time she'd touched her lips to Mad Dog's she'd done it as a thank you. But the resulting zing of sensations quickly turned the thank you kiss into something entirely different.

When Mad Dog kissed her, her heart stopped, her lungs ceased to function and her soul melted into him.

She forgot to breathe.

What had started as a union of two fighters, willing to sacrifice whatever it took to bring a terrorist to justice, had changed into something else.

They both still wanted to complete the mission, but their professional relationship had morphed into an off-the-record, hotter-than-sin attraction Jolie couldn't resist. And from Mad Dog's kiss, he was obviously finding it hard to resist as well.

His tongue traced the seam of her lips, pressing gently, questioningly.

Jolie opened to him, meeting his tongue with her own in a long, tender caress that started slow and sensuous.

Mad Dog's hands slid down her neck. He cupped the back of her head and pulled her closer, deepening their connection.

Jolie threaded her hands into his hair, liking the rich texture and the thickness between her fingers. Slowly, she slipped her palms over his shoulders and down his arms, measuring the hardness of his muscles. Every time he moved they rippled beneath her fingertips.

Never had she felt this drawn to a man. When he'd leaped out of the truck in an attempt to tackle the man on the motorcycle, her heart had jumped into her throat. At that moment, she'd thought the man had to be insane.

But then, SEALs were trained warriors. He'd failed in his first attempt, then rolled to his feet and tried again. The man was fierce…unstoppable.

But when the gang member had pulled his gun, Jolie knew she couldn't stand by and do nothing. Mad Dog was outnumbered. He couldn't fight the whole gang, or see in all directions at once.

That's when she'd fired her first shot, taking out the man who'd aimed his weapon at Mad Dog. She hadn't fired with the intention to kill. Instead, she'd hit him in the arm. If he'd been more of a threat, she'd have killed him without hesitation.

She blamed her kiss on the wave of adrenaline still coursing through her veins. What else could have made her stand on her toes and press her lips to his? He was her partner, not her lover.

But when Mad Dog kissed her, he shattered her reasoning and sent her into a tailspin of vibrant sensations that culminated in her kissing him back.

She ran her hands down his back and into his jean's back pockets, liking the firmness of his ass beneath her palms, wondering what it would feel like naked.

Though her knees grew weak and her lungs protested the need for air, she regretted when Mad Dog leaned back, breaking their connection.

He swept a strand of her hair behind her ear. "I wish I could forget the world and do this forever."

She sighed and nodded. "But we have work to do. And my house…" The world came back in a rush. "I need to see what damage they've done."

She started for the barn door.

Mad Dog snagged her arm and pulled her back into his embrace. "I'd like to think this isn't over. Just delayed."

Her heart pounded against her ribs, and her pulse winged through her veins. "We'll see."

"We'll see?" He chuckled. "What kind of a response is that?"

She bit down on her bottom lip, afraid to smile and encourage him when she should be keeping her distance. God, but she wanted him closer. "What's happening between us…" she shook her head. "It shouldn't. It's destined for heartache."

"On my side or yours?" He brushed his thumb down

the side of her cheek and softly across her lips. "I suspect on my side."

She wanted to argue that it would be on her side, but she was afraid. Afraid of what she was feeling so soon after meeting the man. "It can't be real. What we're feeling. It's too soon."

He pulled her close, his hard erection pressing against her belly. "It's real. But you're right. It's too soon. You need time. And I need to give it to you." He let go of her waist and stepped back, letting her arms slip through his fingers until he grasped her hand. "But, this isn't where it ends, sweetheart." He leaned close until his mouth was a breath away from her ear. "This is where it begins."

He left her standing in the barn and walked out into the open.

Jolie gave herself several more seconds to drag air into her lungs and calm her racing pulse. The man had her all knots inside. How could she think with him kissing and confusing her? She was a goddamn CIA agent, not a teenager on her first date. Hell, they hadn't even gone on a date. They'd only known each other for an afternoon, a night and part of a day.

"This is wrong. So wrong," she muttered.

"I can hear you," Mad Dog said. He appeared in the doorway, his face a dark blob with the sun on his back. "And it's only wrong if you make it wrong. From where I stand, it felt pretty right to me." He held out his hand. "Come on, the coast is clear. Let's see what damage they did."

She knew she was in trouble, but couldn't help it.

Giving herself over to him, Jolie placed her hand in his and let him lead her up the rise to the ranch house.

Jolie's heart dropped into her belly. The paint on the wall could be painted over, but the symbols were what worried her. The swastikas in bright red indicated what he'd feared. The motorcycle gang was indeed the gang terrorizing Eagle Rock. And they'd decided to target her.

As if she didn't have enough going wrong in her life with Nadir, the radicalized ISIS terrorist, gunning for her.

Mad Dog glanced at her, his brow dipping. "Are you sure you're all right?"

"It's just paint," she said.

She'd grown up in the house, had a good childhood and loved her father. The desecration hurt, but it wasn't the end of the world. "My father always told me not to cry over things that could be fixed. Just fix it."

Mad Dog chuckled. "I think I would have liked your father."

"You would have. Everyone did." Jolie shook her head. "Except the one who shot him."

"In all the people the authorities interviewed, did they find anyone who would have wanted your father dead?"

She shook her head. "No one. It baffled the police. It's the reason the case was never solved. I think the entire county showed up for his funeral. There wasn't a dry eye in the chapel." Jolie climbed the steps of the back porch and touched the red paint. "It's already dry."

"We can paint over it."

"The place needs a fresh coat anyway before I can sell it."

"You're convinced you'll sell?" he asked.

She shrugged. "I have no reason to come back. I should have sold the ranch before I left. I'm sure I could get a pile of money for the place, what with all the people from California searching for a place to get away from the noise of the cities."

"Are you staying on after we resolve the situation with Nadir?"

She nodded. "Long enough to get this place ready for sale. Not a moment longer."

"Why?" He climbed the steps to stand beside her and took her hand. "Because of all the memories?"

She nodded, her fingers curling around his. "The thought of someone else living here makes me sad. My mother and father loved this house and the land. They talked about raising their babies and grandbabies here."

"Then your mother died..." he said softly, in a way that encouraged her to continue.

"Dad said they'd always wanted half a dozen children." Jolie laughed, the sound sad and lonely, even to her own ears. "Mom couldn't have any more after me."

"Then your father died..."

"And took with him any reason for me to stay in the back of beyond." She turned to stare out at the pasture. "Why would I stay when my job is with the CIA? I have to be in Virginia, or wherever else they send me. I don't have time to come out to Montana and run a ranch."

"Will you make a lifetime commitment out of the CIA?" Mad Dog asked.

"Why not? I need a job, and I can't run a ranch by myself."

"What if you got married and had children of your own?"

She snorted. "I'm an assassin. That scares most men."

He pulled her into the circle of his arms. "Not me."

Jolie leaned into him. "I've seen the videos of what SEALs have to go through in training. You're a special kind of crazy to do that."

Mad Dog laughed out loud. "Okay, then. I'm crazy, and you're badass. A lethal combination."

"An impossible combination." She walked out of his embrace, determined to put distance between her and her burgeoning desire. Hell, it followed her, swelling in her like magma in a volcano. "Why would the gang target my house and me? Do you think they've been recruited by Nadir?"

He shook his head, frowning. "I'd like to talk with Hank. He and my boss have been talking. Someone's bound to have seen some chatter on the internet."

"My land line was disconnected eight years ago, and cell phones are useless this far out." She pushed a hand through her hair. "I'd like to look around the ranch before dark." Jolie faced Mad Dog. "Can we visit Hank after dark or tomorrow?"

Mad Dog hesitated, and then nodded. "Sure. Though we still need to report the gang attack."

"And we will." Her lips twitched. "Unless you want to put off your first riding lesson."

He held up his hand. "No, no. I'm game, if you are."

"It's been a while since I rode a horse. I have to tell

you, it takes some getting used to. I'll be as sore as you are tomorrow."

"I doubt it," Mad Dog muttered, rubbing his thigh.

"How's the leg?"

"Fine," he said through clenched teeth. "Let's saddle up those ponies and ride out into the sunset, or whatever the hell cowboys do."

Jolie laughed all the way to the barn, her anger over the damage to the house mellowing as she went.

She led Topper, the bay gelding, out of his stall and tied him to a ring affixed to one of the support timbers. Then she led out Butterscotch, the palomino mare, and tied her off to another pole.

"Just do what I do," she said and entered the tack room, hefted a saddle from the saddletree, snagged a blanket and carried them out to her horse. The blanket went on first, and then the saddle.

Mad Dog followed her move for move.

She gave him pointers about placement of the saddle and blanket and showed him how to cinch the girth around the horse's belly. "Tighten it more than once. Sometimes, the horse blows out his belly. If you're not careful, you'll find the saddle, and the person in it, sliding sideways off the horse."

Once they had both horses saddled, Jolie helped Mad Dog adjust the stirrups to a length suitable for his long legs. Then it was time for the bridles.

Mad Dog tried to do what Jolie was doing, but the gelding wouldn't open his teeth.

Jolie grinned. "They can be stubborn sometimes. Stick your thumb in the corner of his mouth like this."

She slipped her thumb into the corner of the gelding's mouth. The horse opened his teeth, and she slid the bit to the back of his mouth and the straps over his ears. "Easy," she said.

"If you say so."

"The hard part will be staying in the saddle for more than fifteen minutes." She led her horse toward the door.

"Not so fast." Mad Dog grabbed his reins and hurried out ahead of her, his horse plodding along behind him.

Jolie could get irritated by Mad Dog's insistence on being first out the door, but she found it endearing that he wanted to be sure she was safe. It was nice to be able to rely on someone for a change, instead of being completely self-sufficient. Her father had raised her to stand on her own two feet and operate independently. But he'd also taught her the value of having a partner to help out in tough situations. She had to remind herself this partnership wasn't forever. The thought made her sad.

AFTER A CRASH COURSE in how to mount and post, Mad Dog found himself high on a horse, riding across a pasture into the hills. When the horse was walking, he was fine. Trotting was hell, and galloping felt like he was flying in the wind.

Like Jolie had warned, he was sore as hell in the first fifteen minutes, his tail bone bruised and his legs cramping from trying to figure out the rhythm he needed to employ to save his ass from a thorough beating in the saddle.

He made a mental note to himself to check out what it would take to revive the four-wheelers before the next time they headed out into the hills. Horseback riding was definitely an acquired skill and took time to build up to.

His partner seemed a natural in the saddle. Every move was fluid and graceful. She and the horse seemed to understand what was expected and became like one entity moving together.

Why the hell had Lambert sent him to Montana to help out an agent who was also a cowgirl? What she needed was someone who knew his way around a horse. Not a gimpy dude with no idea how to save his own ass in the saddle.

Maybe Hank had one of his Brotherhood Protectors who'd be a better match to protect Jolie.

As bad as his tailbone hurt, Mad Dog couldn't bring himself to abandon Jolie now. The woman had already earned a special place in his heart. He couldn't leave her now. If anything happened to her, and he wasn't there to stop it, he wouldn't be able to live with himself.

Which left him where he was. In a saddle on a horse that couldn't quite keep up with Butterscotch, praying Jolie would soon turn back and head for the barn.

That didn't seem to be her plan as she led the way deeper into the hills.

Before long, they climbed a steep trail and descended into a narrow canyon with rugged bluffs rising up on either side of the valley between.

A stream ran through the middle of the canyon, the water crystal-clear and sparkling in the afternoon sun.

Jolie stopped her horse beside the stream, swung her leg over the mare's back and dropped to the ground.

Mad Dog did the same and almost fell on his butt when his legs gave out. He held onto the saddle to keep from falling and tried to appear fine when he stared across the horse's back toward Jolie.

"How are you holding up?" she asked, looking as fresh as when she got up that morning.

"Fine," Mad Dog replied though he doubted he'd ever be able to sit again. Thankful for a few minutes respite from riding, he dreaded the time he'd have to climb back into the saddle and continue the torture.

Jolie stared at him through narrowed eyes. "My ass is sore. You're probably hurting by now."

"A little," he owned up.

Jolie snorted. "Yeah." She didn't belabor the point. Instead, she turned toward the bluffs. "The caves Chase was talking about are hidden in these bluffs. If the gang is using them as a meeting place, we should find some evidence."

"And then what?"

"And then we call the sheriff and have him handle it. I'm not here to wrangle a gang. I want them out of the way, so I can corner Nadir when he shows."

"Agreed." Mad Dog stared up at the bluffs. "Are we searching on horseback or on foot?" He prayed she'd say on foot.

"On foot. We can tie the horse to a tree while we explore."

Mad Dog nearly cried in his relief.

After they watered the horses, they tied them to low hanging branches and climbed up a slope, dodging giant boulders to where water had carved holes in the sides of the cliffs.

"We used to play in these caves when I was a kid," Jolie whispered as she eased up the incline.

"Some girls play with dolls," Mad Dog said.

"Not me," Jolie replied. "Not when I had all of this as my playground."

As they neared the top of the incline, a gaping hole opened into a cave.

Mad Dog touched Jolie's arm. "Let me go first."

She didn't argue, but stood back while he entered the cave.

Mad Dog pulled a pen flashlight out of his pocket and shined it into the darkness.

The cave was about the size of a living room and not very deep.

"If I remember correctly, there are deeper caves the farther along we go into the canyon," Jolie said beside him. "Let's keep moving. It'll get dark soon. The mountains knock thirty minutes of daylight off the clock by blocking the sun."

The next couple of caves were like the first—shallow and empty. Jolie and Mad Dog clung to the shadow of the trees, moving quickly and quietly along. As they neared the fourth cave, Mad Dog pointed to the ground. "Tire tracks."

Jolie nodded. "They've been around here." She stared at the trail leading up to the cave. It was narrow but could accommodate a dirt bike. "Think they left someone to guard it?"

"I'd think they would already be shooting at us, if they had," Mad Dog commented. "But let me—"

"—go first," Jolie finished. "I'll cover." She pulled her nine millimeter Glock from her holster and assumed a kneeling position resting her elbow on her knee.

Mad Dog hesitated.

"I'm good," Jolie said. "I won't shoot you in the back...unless you piss me off."

He leaned down and pressed a kiss to the top of her head. "Thanks." And he was off, climbing the hill. Though his leg was sore and his butt was bruised, he moved as quickly as he could. As he neared the top of the trail, he slowed, studying the ground and the trail ahead. Something wasn't right. His gut was screaming at him to back off. In all his years as a SEAL, his instincts had been spot on. Moving even slower, he inched his way along the trail. Something flashed on the ground just as he took his next step.

"Fuck!"

He dove to the side, which happened to be the steep slope off the edge of the path. Half sitting, half sliding on his feet, he descended at break-neck speed. Behind him, the cliff erupted, spewing rocks, gravel and giant boulders.

Mad Dog yelled, "Get out of the way! Run!" He fell back on his bottom and slid faster as the dust and rocks spun up around him.

A giant boulder bounced past him like a child's ball, shaking the earth with every impact.

When he reached the bottom, Mad Dog covered his head and neck with his arms and made a run for it.

Jolie stood several yards away, yelling something at him.

"Run! Run! Run!" he yelled.

She didn't move, waiting for him to reach her side.

He grabbed her arm and dragged her along with him, away from the landslide that was pushing half of the hillside to the bottom.

When they were far enough away that they weren't being pummeled by rocks and gravel, Mad Dog slowed, coughing the dust from his lungs.

Jolie was covered in a thick layer of dirt. All he could see were the whites of her eyes and teeth. "What the hell happened?" she said and coughed up a lungful of dust.

Mad Dog couldn't believe he hadn't seen it sooner. He'd never expected anything like it Stateside. "I hit a trip wire."

CHAPTER 9

By the time they reached the barn, the sun had dropped below the mountain peaks, casting the barn and house in a gray haze. Exhaustion threatened to dull Jolie's senses. She fought back, determined to stay aware and ready for gangs or terrorists. But deep down, she was tired to the bone. All she wanted was a shower and sleep.

As drained as she was, she figured Mad Dog was in worse shape. Having fought off the motorcycle gang, and then slid down a mountainside in an avalanche, his body had to be worse for the wear.

"I can take care of the horses," she offered. "If you want to get the first shower."

He shook his dusty head. "Not leaving you out here alone. Besides, it's faster when we work together."

She didn't waste energy arguing but got to work, stripping the saddle and blanket off Butterscotch. After a quick brush down, she settled the horse in her stall, gave her a bucket of water and another bucket of feed.

Mad Dog deposited two sections of hay in the stall with her and took another two sections to Topper.

When he was done, he checked the yard outside the barn, shining a heavy-duty flashlight all around before declaring the yard safe enough for Jolie.

He hooked his arm around her and hurried her to the house, entering first.

Jolie liked that he checked every room and the basement before he allowed her free rein of her home. As tired as she was, she should be irritated. But no one had cared as much about her safety since her father died. It was a good feeling she hadn't realized she'd missed.

She peeled off her leather jacket and hung it on a hook next to the back door. It needed a thorough cleaning, but would have to wait until the morning.

"Do you want to shower first?" she asked.

He shook his head. "You go. You have to be exhausted."

"You too. And that leg must hurt. I might have something for you." She left him in the kitchen, entered her bedroom and rummaged through her toiletries kit for over-the-counter painkillers.

When she returned to the kitchen, she handed him the pills. "Take these. They might help the leg and the sore tailbone."

He tossed the pills to the back of his throat and swallowed.

Jolie raised her eyebrows. "Really? No water?" She

shook her head, reached for a glass and filled it with water from the tap. "Here. Wash them down."

He complied. "Now, hurry into the shower, before I change my mind and race you for it."

Jolie turned toward the hallway and took a step, her pulse picking up. Before she could think too hard, she spun back around. "We can shower together," she blurted. As soon as the words were out of her mouth, she wished she could take them back.

What the hell was she thinking? Just because he'd kissed her didn't mean he wanted more. Had she read too much into that one kiss? Heat rose in her cheeks, burning all the way out to the tips of her ears.

For a long moment, Mad Dog didn't say a word, but stared at her.

"It's okay," Jolie muttered. "Don't feel obligated. Sometimes, I don't know when to keep my big mouth shut. No worries. Carry on with whatever you were doing. I'll slink off into the bathroom and hurry up so you can get your shower next."

Mad Dog closed the distance between them in two large steps, grabbed the back of her neck and crushed his mouth to hers in a hard, glorious kiss.

When he broke it off, he whispered against her lips. "Anyone ever tell you that you talk too much?"

"No," she said. "And normally I don't. But you make me crazy."

He slipped his arm around her dusty, dirty body and pulled her against him. His erection pressed into her belly. "You make me crazy, too."

She licked her dry lips, tasting the dust on them and not caring. "Does this mean we're showering together?"

"Damn right, we are." Mad Dog scooped her up into his arms and marched down the hallway to the bathroom where he set her on her feet.

"I'm capable of getting places on my own," she protested. "Your leg—"

Mad Dog pressed a finger to her lips, stemming her flow of words. "Shh."

Jolie clamped her lips shut and pressed a kiss to his finger.

Then he tugged her shirt free of her jeans and up over her head, ignoring the buttons that could have been loosened first.

Jolie didn't complain. The way he did it was faster and got the job done. She kicked off her boots, slinging them to the side.

Mad Dog toed off his boots as well, dragged his T-shirt over his head and dropped it on the floor. A puff of dust rose around it.

Jolie could only imagine how awful she looked, caked in dirt from the hillside explosion. But she didn't care. And Mad Dog didn't seem deterred by her filthy body. As he peeled the layers of clothing off, his gaze grew more intense.

He unbuttoned her jeans, slipped the zipper down, and then dragged them over her hips and down her thighs.

Jolie stepped free of the denim and stood in her panties and bra in front of the hottest guy she'd ever seen.

Shirtless, the man's muscles were hard, corded and rippled with every move.

She reached for the button on his jeans, pushed it through the hole and eased his zipper down. He was hard and stiff and naked underneath. When she parted his fly, his cock sprang free, long and thick.

Jolie took him into her palm and wrapped her hand around his length.

He covered her hand with his. "Let's take it to the shower." Then he reached behind her, switched on the water and adjusted the temperature until it was warm.

Once again, he swept her off her feet.

Jolie curled an arm around his neck and enjoyed the feeling of being light and delicate. No man had ever made her feel as insanely feminine as this one.

Mad Dog stepped into the tub with her before he lowered her feet to the ground. He lifted the bottle of shampoo she'd left there the night before, squeezed some into his hand and turned her back to him. With gentle hands, he lathered her hair, massaged her scalp and rinsed the suds. The lather slipped down her neck and over her shoulders, making rivulets in the layers of dust covering her body.

Mad Dog reached for the bar of soap in the soap dish, worked up a lather and started at Jolie's neck and worked his way downward, skimming his hands over her shoulders and arms and finally to the swell of her hips. Then his hands circled around and came up her torso to her breasts, cleaning and rubbing them with the slick soap.

Jolie leaned against him, a moan rising up her throat

as his cock pressed into the crease of her buttocks. Her body was on fire. She was surprised steam didn't rise from her skin.

Frustrated by having her back to him when all she wanted to do was touch, feel and taste every part of him, Jolie turned.

She repeated the favor, washing his hair, scrubbing the dust and grit from his scalp. All the while, his shaft pressed against her belly, hard, thick and insistent. Jolie could hardly wait to have him inside her.

Mad Dog leaned back, ducking his head beneath the spray and washing the soapsuds from his hair.

While he rinsed, Jolie worked up bubbles with the bar of soap and ran her palms across his body, starting at the neck and working her way over his broad shoulders. Her fingers circled and massaged, running across his chest, stopping long enough to tweak his little brown nipples.

The shower spray rinsed away the soap, leaving his skin clean and tempting.

Jolie leaned close and sucked one of his wet nipples into her mouth. She rolled the nub between her teeth and nipped gently.

"Hey," he jerked back, out of range of her teeth.

She giggled and slipped her soapy hands down his torso and lower until they bumped into his stiffened cock.

Mad Dog sucked in a sharp breath, closed his eyes and tipped his head back. "You don't know how good that feels."

"Mmm. I have an idea." She smiled and curled her

fingers around him, loving that she was responsible for how hard he was. It gave her a feeling of power and awe.

He captured her chin in his hand and tipped her face up to his, water splattering them as the shower ran on. "Are you sure this is what you want?"

Her hand tightened ever so slightly around him. "Never more certain in my life."

He smiled and kissed the tip of her nose. "Why the change of heart?"

Jolie laughed. "Why all the questions? Isn't it enough I want you?"

Mad Dog brushed her lips with his. "You know how much I desire you. What I don't want is for you to wake up in the morning full of regret."

"I won't wake up full of regret. I'm a grown-ass woman, capable of pleasuring myself. I know the difference between okay and wow. I'm looking for wow. It's been a long time since I've had wow."

He chuckled. "Then prepare yourself to be *wowed*."

MAD DOG RAN his hands over Jolie's ass and down to the back of her thighs, scooped her up into his arms and pressed her back to the shower wall.

Jolie wrapped her legs around his waist and her arms around his neck.

He touched his cock to her entrance but stopped short. Damn. Why didn't he think of it before? Mad Dog sighed. "I don't have protection."

"What?" Jolie leaned her head against the wall and

moaned. "I'm having regrets. Tell me you don't have them here, now, but that you have them in the other room, in your wallet or something?"

He shook his head. "Sorry. I didn't come to Montana to fuck my new partner."

She wrinkled her nose. "You weren't much of a Boy Scout, were you?"

"Normally, I am always prepared. But I wasn't expecting this." He nudged her with his cock again, and then unwound her legs from around his waist. "But that doesn't mean I can't satisfy you." Mad Dog grabbed the bar of soap and lathered up again. "Let's finish up in here, I have plans for later."

They soaped each other's bodies all the way down their legs, rinsing the last of the dust and dirt down the drain. The mud they'd made to start with, cleared, and was sucked down with the soap suds. By the time they were done, the water was chilly and gooseflesh rose on their skin.

Mad Dog stepped out first, grabbed a towel and held Jolie's hand as she swung her leg over the edge of the tub. He took his time drying her body, exploring as he dried every inch.

He waited impatiently while she dried his body, wishing he had thought to pack a condom. The evening would have gone a lot differently had he come prepared.

When they were both dry, Mad Dog leaned forward, ready to scoop her up in his arms.

Jolie held up a hand. "I can walk."

"And take all the fun out of it? No way." He swung

her naked body up in the air and pressed her close to him. "See? Isn't that better?"

"Better than when you carried me all dusty and dirty into the shower." She trailed her fingers across his naked chest. "Are you sure you didn't bring a condom? I'd check my father's nightstand, but eight-year-old protection could be suspect."

"Don't worry about me. I have plans for you. The night is far from over."

Jolie's body quivered in his arms.

He carried her across the hallway to her bedroom and sat her on the edge of the bed.

Her gaze swept over him from his eyes, down his chest, to pause on his staff, jutting outward, eager and ready for more than he could promise that night. Her tongue darted out and swiped across her lips. She reached out to touch him.

His cock jerked in response. Mad Dog moaned and captured her hand in his. "Not yet. You first."

"But I want to touch you, too," she said.

"Later, if you have any energy left." He grinned and turned her palm up to press a kiss against it. Then he laid her back on the bed and pinned her wrists above her head. "I want to make you scream with your release," he whispered against her lips, and then crushed her mouth with his.

She opened to him, thrusting her tongue against his, twisting and tangling, her body rising from the mattress, her breasts pressing to his chest.

Mad Dog left her mouth and trailed his lips across

her chin and down the long line of her neck to where her pulse beat a rapid tattoo.

She writhed beneath him, a moan rising from deep in her throat.

Inch by inch, he explored her body with his mouth, kissing and flicking his tongue across her collarbone and down to the swells of her breasts. He released his hold on her wrists, captured one breast with his fingers and sucked the other between his lips. While he massaged and tweaked one nipple, he rolled the other between his teeth, flicking his tongue over the hardened bud.

Jolie arched upward, thrusting her breast closer, urging him to take more.

He switched sides and tongued and flicked the other breast, before sucking hard on the nipple.

Eager to taste all of her, he shifted his weight and moved down her body, tonguing a path across her ribs to her bellybutton, and lower, to the fluff of hair at the apex of her thighs.

She stopped writhing, her breath catching and holding, her body tensing.

Mad Dog blew a stream of air over her mons, stirring the curls. Then he dropped over the side of the bed, pressed her knees wide and parted her folds with his thumbs. "I want to taste your desire," he murmured.

Her entrance glistened with her juices, evidence she was as turned on as he was.

He tongued her there, tasting her essence.

She gasped and ran her hand down to her clit, touching the nubbin that was Mad Dog's next goal.

He kissed her hand and moved it to the mound of hair, clearing his path. With a light, flick, he touched his tongue to her clit.

Jolie's body jerked. Her knees rose, spreading wider. "Oh, dear, sweet heaven," she muttered her voice heavy with desire.

Mad Dog swept his tongue the length of that nerve-packed bundle of flesh and sucked it into his mouth.

Fingers threaded into his hair, and Jolie's nails dug into his scalp, pulling him closer.

He licked her again, loving the way her body writhed and twitched, as if she had no control. He smiled and flicked her again.

Jolie was a woman who enjoyed controlling every part of her life.

Mad Dog liked that he made her lose control. With that goal in mind, he slipped his finger into her wet channel and swirled in the warmth and dampness. At the same time, he launched his campaign on her clit, tonguing, flicking and teasing it until she cried out his name.

"Mad Dog! Geez, what you're doing to me?"

He paused long enough to ask, "Want me to stop?"

"Hell, no!" She moaned and raised her hips, urging him to continue.

He did, plying his skills again and again.

Finally, Jolie slapped her hands on the bed beside her, raised her hips and held them high, her body pulsing with her release. "Yeesss!"

Then she sank to the mattress, trembling, a thin sheen of perspiration making her face glow in the light from the nightstand. "That was...I've never...holy hell." She laughed and tossed her head back and forth.

Mad Dog scooted her more fully onto the mattress and climbed up to lie beside her. "You've never what?"

She cupped his cheek in her palm. "Never felt that good in my entire life."

"Then I did it right." He winked and kissed her lips.

"Mmm. I love that you taste like me." Jolie kissed him, thrust her tongue between his teeth and swept across his tongue in a long, warm caress. Then she rolled over on top of him and planted her hands on either side of his face. "Now, it's my turn."

"Hmm. I like it when the woman takes command."

"Then you're going to like this." She pressed her lips to his forehead, the tip of his nose, each cheek and, finally, his lips. After a long, slow kiss, she slid her mouth along the stubble of his chin.

"Sorry," he apologized. "I'll shave next time."

"No, don't," she said, her voice throaty. "I like how abrasive it is against my skin. It drives me wild."

Note to self, don't shave for her. She likes it rough.

This woman was perfect in every way.

Taking her time, she worked her way down his sinewy neck and along the muscular planes of his shoulders and chest. She paused long enough to roll the little brown nipples between her teeth, one at a time, nipping and flicking them until he grabbed her ass and moved her further down his body.

She complied. He suspected because that was her ultimate intention.

Jolie kissed, tongued or nipped each rib on her way

133

south, culminating at that part of him ready to explode at her touch.

Straddling his legs, she wrapped her warm hands around him and slid them down to the base and back up again.

Mad Dog sucked in a long, steadying breath, counted to ten and prayed he didn't lose it too soon. He wanted this to last. Hell, he wanted to be inside her, fucking her until she came with him.

She stroked him, circling and running her hands up his length and back down, and then curling them around his balls and rolling them between her fingers.

"You keep that up, and I won't last long," he said through gritted teeth.

"Oh, then I'll stop." She pulled her hands away.

He leaned up on his elbows. "Good God, woman, don't stop!"

She laughed and resumed her massage. Jolie leaned over and kissed the tip of his dick.

Mad Dog dropped to his back and closed his eyes, praying she'd do more, but unwilling to ask for it. If she wanted to give him a blow job, it had to be up to—

Warm, wet lips wrapped around his cock and sucked.

He opened his eyes and stared down at the top of Jolie's bright, strawberry-blond head.

She took all of him, until the tip bumped the back of her throat.

When she came back up, he groaned and followed her, thrusting up into her mouth.

Her chuckle warmed his cock. Her teeth skimmed

the sides, hard, but careful, creating an even more erotic sensation than just her soft lips.

Mad Dog grabbed her hair and held her, twisting his fingers in the soft strands. "You don't have to do this," he whispered.

She came off him and replied, "I want to." Then she was back on him, fucking him with her mouth. Up and down, rolling his balls in her hands, faster and faster, until Mad Dog could contain himself no longer.

He tightened his grip on her hair and pulled her off, just as he came, his seed spilling out over his belly.

Jolie sat back on his legs, a smile spreading across her face. "Next time, bring a condom so we can finish this."

CHAPTER 10

JOLIE LAY in bed for a long time, staring up at the ceiling, barely visible in the starlight edging through the curtains over her window.

How had a mission to catch a terrorist ended up in her bedroom with her assigned partner? Throughout her career, she'd been very careful to maintain her distance and keep it professional between herself and any partner she was assigned.

But Mad Dog was different. He wasn't an agent in the CIA. Hell, Jolie wasn't even sure what agency he belonged to.

At that moment, past midnight, satiated, warm and feeling pretty damned safe in his arms, she didn't care if he was the enemy. She'd switch sides just to do what they did again.

But definitely with a condom next time. Though she'd come on a screaming orgasm, their lovemaking wasn't quite complete. She wanted to feel that thick, hot cock buried deep inside her, filling a place that had been empty for far too long.

She must have drifted off, because when she opened her eyes, sunlight streamed through the open curtains and warmed the foot of her bed.

As the memory of the night before washed over her, she turned toward…an empty pillow.

What the hell?

Jolie sat up straight, the quilt falling down to her waist, exposing her naked skin to the chill morning air.

Had she imagined making love with Mad Dog?

Her clit tingled, and parts of her body burned from where his light beard had scraped her skin. And there was a dent in the pillow beside her.

She threw herself onto it and inhaled the scent of Mad Dog—the clean, soapy, man-smell that was unique to the former SEAL.

"Feel like having some eggs without bacon?" His rich, deep voice warmed the room and made her shiver at the same time.

Jolie grabbed the quilt and pulled it over her naked breasts before sitting to greet him. "You're up early," she said.

The warm, rich aroma of coffee wafted in her direction from the tray the man carried.

She smiled. "You made coffee?"

"Figured you could use some. I know I'm not much good before my first jolt of caffeine." He set the tray on top of the dresser and carried her cup to her. "Start with this. I have scrambled eggs and toast for your second course."

Jolie, tucked the quilt under her arms, wrapped her hands around the mug and drew in a deep breath, absorbing the caffeinated drink through her other senses before taking her first sip. The hot brew burned her tongue and all the way down the back of her throat. But it was heaven. "You're an angel of mercy."

He chuckled. "I don't know about that. I made coffee and eggs out of purely selfish reasons. I needed fuel for my body."

"I don't care what your reasons were, you brought me a cup of Joe." She took another sip, smaller this time to keep from scorching every last taste bud. "All that matters is that I have coffee."

"Save room for eggs." He retrieved the tray from the dresser and laid it across her lap.

Jolie struggled to hold the mug in her hands, the quilt beneath her arms and balance the tray across her lap. When the quilt slipped to her waist, she nearly spilled her coffee, and she rocked the tray.

"Sweetheart, it's not like I haven't seen them already." Mad Dog winked and retrieved the coffee mug from her hands, set it on the tray and carried the tray to the dresser.

"I don't normally flash a man this early in the morning," she muttered.

His chuckle filled the air as he pulled an oversized T-shirt from his duffel bag and tossed it to her. "Wear that, if it makes you more comfortable."

She shrugged into the shirt, inhaling the scent she associated with Mad Dog. With her upper half covered, she felt a little less exposed and vulnerable in front of the SEAL. "I can finish breakfast in the kitchen," she said and flung back the quilt and tangled sheets.

The hem of the T-shirt fell to her knees, covering everything that mattered. But knowing he'd worn the shirt made the fabric brushing against her set her skin on fire and her core tighten. What would it be like to wake up and make love with this man, first thing every day?

Strangely shy after sleeping with him, Jolie couldn't quite meet his gaze. Instead, she tried to reach around him for the tray, only to be captured in his embrace and pulled tightly against his solid, muscular body.

Oh, yeah, it would be heaven to wake up in this man's arms every day.

He tipped up her chin. "No regrets?"

She shook her head, her cheeks heating at the memory of how he'd gone down on her and made her scream out his name. "You?"

He grunted. "No way. My plan is to stop at whatever store there is in town and stock up on condoms this morning—after we visit the sheriff's office."

Jolie liked the sound of stocking up on condoms, but mention of the sheriff made her frown. "You're right. They need to know what happened out here yesterday. I would have called, if we'd a phone line."

"Exactly. The sheriff needs to know the gang has been meeting in the caves on your property, and that they attacked you and your home."

"I suppose so," she said, sighing. "They'll be all over the place investigating."

"We can give our deposition, stop at the store for

bacon and other items, and then head out to Hank's. I want to know what's happening on the internet."

"If I stay here much longer, I'll need to get connected," Jolie noted.

Mad Dog released her and lifted the tray. "Come on, let's get you fed and dressed. We have a long day ahead. And we still don't know where our terrorist is hiding."

"Do you suppose it was a long shot, thinking he'd follow me out here?"

"We won't know until we do some digging. That's where I hope Hank or his contacts will be of use."

In the kitchen, Jolie sat at the table, aware of the fact she was naked beneath the T-shirt, while Mad Dog was fully clothed. She tried to concentrate on the eggs, toast and coffee but gave up halfway through breakfast and carried her plate and mug to the sink.

Mad Dog stepped up behind her. "I can wash those."

Having him so close was driving her crazy. Jolie wanted to lean back against his body and...

Jolie washed her dish in the soapy water in the sink, rinsed and set the plate in the drainer. When she turned, he was standing there, his gaze burning into hers.

"Do you realize what a turn-on it is to see you in one of my T-shirts, knowing you're naked beneath it?"

She laughed, the sound coming out breathy. "So, it's not just me?"

He pulled her into his arms and reached beneath the hem of the shirt. Mad Dog splayed his warm hands across her buttocks, then slid them up her sides to cup her breasts. "You're derailing every one of my brain cells."

"I'm finding it…very…difficult to focus on anything when you hold me like this." She leaned her breasts into his open palms. Jolie closed her eyes and tilted back her head, loving the way his hands massaged her nipples. "When did you say we're stopping by the store?"

Mad Dog laughed out loud and bent to capture her lips in a soul-defining kiss. When he released her, he smacked his palm to her ass. "Get dressed. We have work to do."

Right. Work. As she hurried back through the house, Jolie glanced out the windows. Where was Nadir? Had he found her yet? Would he come to her house and try to kill her, or would he send his minions to do his dirty work?

Dressed in jeans, a white blouse, boots and a black leather jacket, Jolie pulled her hair back into a ponytail and secured it with a rubber band. She released the magazine in the handle of her pistol, checked to see it was full, and slammed it home. Safety on, she shoved it into the shoulder holster beneath her jacket.

A glance in the mirror showed a determined woman, with a strange glow in her cheeks. Is that what it looked like to be thoroughly satisfied in bed? A smile spread across her face as she left her bedroom and joined Mad Dog on the porch.

"Ready?" he asked.

To go back to bed and finish what they'd started the night before? Hell, yeah!

"Ready," she said and walked out to his truck. "Want me to drive?" she asked.

He shook his head. "I've got this."

He held the door for her and helped her up into the passenger seat. Then he rounded the front hood and slid behind the wheel.

When he put his key in the ignition and turned it, nothing happened.

Something triggered in Jolie's gut. Blood shot through her veins, and her heart slammed into her ribs.

Before Mad Dog could turn the key again, Jolie put a hand over his.

"Get out of the truck," she said, her voice low, tense.

"What?"

"Get out of the truck, now!" She flung her door open and threw herself out of the truck.

Mad Dog did the same, only a split second behind her.

"Run!" she shouted and raced for the corner of the house.

The world behind her exploded, the force blasting her forward into the bushes surrounding the porch.

For a long moment, she lay with her face to the ground, waiting for any secondary explosions. *Stay down, Caleb. Stay down*, she thought, unable to scream out the warning, because she had yet to catch her breath.

A moment later, the second explosion, rocked the ground beneath her and spewed smoke and flames into the air.

Glass shattered, and the acrid scent of burning fuel filled the air.

Jolie pushed to her knees and sucked in air, coughed and sucked in more. When she could finally stand, she glanced toward the truck, searching for Mad Dog.

"Jolie?" his voice came to her over the crackle of the fire. "Jolie?"

Mad Dog rounded the side of the house, spotted her and ran toward her, swinging wide of the flaming heap that had been his truck.

She met him halfway and flung herself into his arms. "I thought you didn't make it out fast enough."

"I thought the same about you. I couldn't get to you." He held her at arm's length. "Were you hurt?"

Jolie shook her head and smoothed her hands over his chest. "Were you?"

"No. Thanks to you." He turned toward his ruined truck. "How did you know?"

"When the truck didn't start, something inside told me to get out." She leaned into him. "I'm sorry about your truck."

"I'm sorry I didn't figure it out first. You could have died in that explosion." His arm tightened around her.

"The important thing is that we're both alive." Her ears still rang, but neither one of them had wounds from flying shrapnel.

"We can take my SUV to town," Jolie offered.

Mad Dog frowned. "After we inspect it thoroughly."

Jolie laughed, the sound dull and flat, even to her own ears. "Damn right."

"The question is, who set the explosives? Nadir or our industrious gang? They could well have done it, given that they booby-trapped the cave in the hills."

"We need to bring the sheriff in on this," Jolie said.

"And we probably need to let him know about Nadir. That way they can be on the lookout for strangers fitting his description."

After a thorough inspection of her SUV that she'd parked out by the barn, they didn't find any sign of tampering or explosives.

Jolie tried to insist on starting the engine with Mad Dog standing far enough away he wouldn't be injured in the blast. "Nadir is my bad guy. If he's aiming for me, let it be me."

"I don't give a rat's ass if Nadir is after you or me. I'm starting that engine. Not you." He held his hand out for the key, blocking her from getting into the vehicle.

After a stubborn second or two, Jolie handed him the key. "Fine. Blow yourself up."

He waved her to a safe distance and slipped behind the wheel.

Jolie held her breath, her heart stopping as she waited.

A moment later, the engine roared to life. Nothing exploded excerpt for the air from Jolie's lungs.

"Thank God," she said and climbed into the passenger seat.

Mad Dog grinned, and then laughed. "You should have seen your face when it actually started."

She slapped his shoulder, the weight of the moment lifting from her shoulders. "It's not funny." But she laughed, too. Tension made her do strange things. Jolie was glad the morning hadn't turned out worse than it had. So, the truck was destroyed.

They were still alive. Now, they just had to find the bastard who'd tried to kill them.

MAD DOG COULD KICK HIMSELF. He'd been sent out to help Jolie find and remove Nadir from circulation as a terrorist on home soil. So far, his batting record sucked.

He'd almost gotten himself killed three times and Jolie twice. Perhaps the Navy had been right to medically retire him. Why Lambert had hired him as a Sleeper SEAL wasn't clear. His boss must have seen more in him than he was seeing in himself.

Jolie had saved his ass twice now. He hoped he could return the favor before something awful happened.

He drove to town without uttering a word, his mind on what had almost happened and what could still take place. He focused on situational awareness. Making love to Jolie should be the last thing on his mind. But it wasn't. And it quite possibly could have gotten them both killed.

He considered contacting Lambert and bowing out of this gig. Jolie needed someone who had his head in the game, and who was physically capable of protecting her should the need arise.

Call him a dumbass, call him stupid, but he couldn't bear the idea of someone else taking over this operation. What if they had no more luck then he had keeping Jolie safe? What if Jolie took a hit because he wasn't there to take the bullet for her?

The answer to his problem was that he'd have to keep his dick in his pants until this was all over. Then, and only then, could he consider making love, touching or kissing Jolie. From now until Nadir or whoever else was harassing and trying to kill Jolie was neutralized, Mad Dog had to remain hands-off of the CIA agent.

He made their first stop the sheriff's office. The sooner the state crime lab got involved investigating the explosives the better.

Jolie entered first and stopped in front of a big man wearing a sheriff's star. "Sheriff Barron?"

The man turned and frowned. "Do I..." His face broke out in a huge grin. "Jolie Richards? Is that you?" He engulfed her in a bear hug so tight he lifted her off the ground. "I heard you were back in town. Why didn't you tell me you were coming? The missus will want to bake a cake or something." He set her back on her feet and stared at her, his smile intact. "You're a sight for sore eyes, girl. Where have you been keeping yourself?"

"I got a job on the east coast," she said. "I'm back in town to clean up the old place and put it up for sale."

The sheriff's smile faded, and he shook his head. "Now, that's news I didn't want to hear. I had high hopes you'd come back to the ranch to live. Your daddy loved that place."

"My job is back east. I can't keep up with the ranch and my work. The place needs someone fulltime." She stepped back and waved toward Mad Dog. "Sheriff, this is Caleb Maddox, my fiancé."

The sheriff held out his hand. "You have to be someone special to snag this girl. She's a keeper. A chip off the old block."

Mad Dog shook the man's hand, gratified to find the

sheriff had a strong grip that brooked no argument and showed no softness. His open face and friendly manner wouldn't be misconstrued with weakness. "She's special, all right. I knew it from the very beginning."

Jolie touched the sheriff's arm. "Could we speak to you in private?"

The sheriff's brow knit. "Certainly, come back to my office. Can I offer you a cup of coffee?"

"No, thank you," Jolie answered. She followed him down a hallway and turned into his office.

Mad Dog closed the door once they were all inside.

The sheriff waved them to the seats across from his desk and sank into his office chair. "What's wrong?"

Jolie shot a glance at Mad Dog, but took the lead, telling the sheriff about her conversation with Deputy Wells, the motorcycle riders, the cave and the two explosions. When she was done, she sat back and folded her hands in her lap. "And one other thing..."

The sheriff shoved a hand through his graying hair. "As if that wasn't enough?"

"This is confidential." She paused.

Sheriff held up a hand as if swearing in court. "Whatever you say in this office, stays in this office."

She nodded. "I work with the CIA."

The older man's lips twitched, and then stretched into a grin. "I knew you were destined for great things." He shot a glance toward Mad Dog. "This little lady was the best shot in all of the tri-county area. Could fire anything from any position and hit it dead on." He returned his attention to Jolie. "So, what's got your knickers in a twist?"

"I have a radicalized terrorist on my tail. I came here to *unofficially* smoke him out on my old stomping grounds. Hopefully, away from a crowded city where others could be caught up in the crossfire."

"You think he might be responsible for the troubles out at your place?"

"I'm not sure if he's had contact with the local gang. If he has, it increases my exposure and makes it more difficult for me to single him out."

Mad Dog sat forward. "We think the gang was responsible for the explosion in the cave. We know they damaged the house and were the ones raising hell on motorcycles, but we don't know if they were the ones to set the explosives in my truck."

"They could have, given they knew how to set an explosion with a tripwire," Jolie said. "But we can't be sure."

"I'll have the state crime lab team come out to investigate and ask them to put a rush on the job."

"If you think for a moment that I've put anyone in this town in danger by being here, tell me," Jolie said. "I'll leave and take my terrorist with me. I just need a couple more days to see if I can get him to show himself."

"You're playing with fire, Jolie," the sheriff said. "Are you sure you'll be safe out there on your ranch? Do you want me to send a unit out to stand guard 24/7?"

Jolie smiled toward Mad Dog. "I have my fiancé. He's a trained Navy SEAL. He'll have my six."

Sheriff Barron turned to Mad Dog, his gaze sweeping his sturdy frame. "Is that right?"

"Yes, sir. I'll do my best to keep Jolie safe."

"Good. If you need anything, just give me a call."

Jolie shook her head. "No landline out there."

"I hadn't thought about that. I'll have a unit check on you on a random basis."

"That would be nice." Jolie stood. "If you see anyone new in town, let me know. I expect he's not far behind me, if he's not already here."

The sheriff rounded his desk and hugged her again. "I hope you'll reconsider and stay in Eagle Rock. We could use more good people like you two."

"Thank you," Jolie said. "Give your wife my love. I'll try to get by to pay my respects—after I've solved my problem, not sooner."

He nodded. "I understand."

Mad Dog shook the older man's hand. "Thank you for taking time to hear us out."

"I'll be out this morning to look around, and I'll come out again when the crime lab team gets here. Where are you headed now?"

"We wanted to pay a visit to an old friend," Jolie said. "Hank Patterson. You don't happen to know where we can find him, do you?"

The sheriff wrote out an address and sketched a drawing of the roads they should take to get there.

"Thank you, Sheriff." Jolie led the way out and stopped before exiting the office building, allowing Mad Dog to go first.

"You're catching on," he whispered as he passed her.

"I know when to choose my battles," she retorted.

Mad Dog stepped out of the building with a grin on

his face. The woman had pluck and attitude. She'd need it over the next few days. The not knowing part was the hardest. They might not see Nadir coming until he showed up in their faces. They had to be prepared for anything. From what Lambert had said, Nadir was also very good at recruiting people to do his bidding. They might not know who was after Jolie until it was too late.

With the eye of a trained combat veteran, Mad Dog scanned the parking lot, neighboring buildings and rooftops. When he was certain no one was lying in wait to pick off Jolie, he allowed her to exit the building, wrapped as much of his body around her as possible and walked her to the SUV.

Once she was inside, she ducked low in her seat and waited for him to climb in next to her.

"There's a grocery store on the corner of Main and Pine," Jolie pointed out. "We can get the...bacon there."

Her slight hesitation before the word bacon let Mad Dog know she was thinking of the other item he'd wanted to get before their next romp on the mattress.

He didn't say anything, but that next romp was going on hold until they had their terrorist. He'd forgo the condoms until that point to ensure they didn't sacrifice their vigilance. Nadir would be looking for opportunities to do more than sabotage a truck.

Mad Dog wasn't even sure it was safe to return to the house. He'd talk with Hank and ask if there was somewhere else they could go. What they needed was a bomb-sniffing, attack dog to check the house and stand guard at night.

Whoever had set the explosives on his truck had

done it in the night, while Mad Dog and Jolie were otherwise occupied or asleep. The saboteur could just as easily have set explosives around the house and blown them away while they'd slept.

Perhaps Hank had some of his former special operations men who had time to provide security for a fellow SEAL and his woman.

After two explosions, and attacks by a raccoon and a motorcycle gang, this cat was running out of lives to spare.

Mad Dog pulled into the grocery store Jolie had indicated.

"I'll get the groceries." Jolie said. "You don't have to go in."

Like hell he'd stay in the truck. "I'm going in."

Jolie was already out of the truck before he could get around to her side and provide protection.

Frowning, he hurried to her. "Dammit, do you want me to paint a bright red target on you?"

"I looked around as we drove up and didn't observe anyone lurking around the store or perched on any of the nearby rooftops. I'd say it's fairly safe to walk ten feet to the door."

He didn't argue with her, just slipped his arm around her waist and ushered her toward the door, using his body as a shield.

Once they were inside, Jolie snagged a cart and left him as she headed down the canned goods aisle.

Mad Dog headed for the refrigerated meats area and selected a large package of bacon, all the while keeping watch on the entrance and Jolie's location. She'd moved on to the snacks and bread, and then over to milk and eggs.

For a moment, Mad Dog lost sight of her behind a large display rack of brightly colored bouncy balls. He leaned left, and then right, but couldn't see Jolie.

His pulse kicked up a notch even though there was probably a good explanation for why he couldn't see her.

That didn't ease his mind one iota. With the package of bacon in his hand, he hurried toward the front of the store, hoping Jolie was headed that way.

Sure enough, she'd finished on the milk and eggs aisle and had taken her items to the check-out counter.

The store clerk had half of her items bagged and was ringing up the rest when Mad Dog stepped up behind her.

"Did you find everything you needed?" he asked.

She nodded without looking up, her cheeks slightly flushed.

Mad Dog placed the bacon on the conveyor belt, adding it to the other purchases. When Jolie reached into her purse for her credit card, Mad Dog was a step ahead. He handed his card to the clerk and paid for the items.

"You don't have to do that," Jolie protested.

"I'm eating, too, and I'm not paying for the room, so let this be my contribution."

Jolie nodded and quickly gathered bags while Mad Dog signed for the purchase, shoved his credit card back into his wallet and grabbed more bags to carry out to the SUV.

Maybe it was him being overly sensitive about everything related to Jolie, but she was acting strange. The normally, in-control woman was twitchy and avoiding eye-contact.

Perhaps, it was just as well. The mental distance would help him keep his shit together.

At least, he hoped it would.

CHAPTER 11

J olie waited while Mad Dog performed his surveillance of the surrounding area before stepping out of the store. She hoped he hadn't seen what she'd secreted away in the bag, before he'd joined her at the check-out.

As hot as they were in the sack the night before, all she was getting from Mad Dog that morning was stiffness and a hands-off kind of vibe. Had the truck explosion shaken him that much he'd reconsidered making love to her again?

Her chest tightened. That kind of reasoning would explain why he hadn't stocked up on condoms in the store.

Of course, it hadn't stopped her from grabbing a month's supply. It was buried beneath the cheese slices and a loaf of bread. Because he wasn't saying much, Jolie felt the need to fill the silence. "It's cool enough that everything in the vehicle won't melt or spoil anytime soon."

"Good, because we still need to go to Hank's."

Using the directions Sheriff Barron had given them, Mad Dog headed out of town on one of the state highways. Several miles out, he turned to stop at the gate of the White Oak Ranch, lowered the window, punched the intercom button and waited.

A man's voice came over the speaker. "White Oak Ranch, how can I help you?"

"Caleb Maddox and Jolie Richards here to see Hank Patterson."

"One moment."

A long pause ensued, followed by a click, and the gate swung open.

Mad Dog pulled through the open gate and drove the long drive, through a stand of trees and up a hill to a beautiful, sprawling ranch house. Unlike Jolie's older home, this one appeared new. Rock and cedar framed massive windows with views of the scenic Crazy Mountains as a backdrop.

Mad Dog parked beside the house, got out and rounded the SUV to open Jolie's door.

Jolie sat in stunned silence, staring at the home and view. "Wow. This place is beautiful."

"Jolie?" A woman's voice sounded from the porch.

Jolie dropped out of the truck and glanced up to see a beautiful woman who could be none other than the Hollywood mega-star, Sadie McClain. She didn't wear makeup, and her hair hung in disarray around her shoulders, but it was her. This was how Jolie remembered her from their school days.

Sadie balanced a baby girl on her hip as she descended the stairs to the ground. "Jolie Richards? Is that you? I haven't seen you in forever."

Jolie smiled and hurried across the yard to greet her old friend. "Hi, Sadie."

When Sadie reached her, she hugged her with one arm and holding the baby with the other. "Hank said you were in the area, and I'd hoped to see you. Look at you. You're as pretty as ever." She hugged her again. The baby patted Jolie's shoulder and giggled.

Jolie smiled and asked, "Aren't you going to introduce me to this little cutie?"

Sadie laughed. "Jolie, meet Emma. Emma, this is Jolie. Can you say Jolie?"

The baby gurgled something unintelligible and laughed.

Sadie laughed with her. "She's trying to form words but hasn't quite mastered the concept. I'm sure once she starts talking, there'll be no shutting her up." Sadie didn't seem to mind, she hugged Emma to her and kissed her with a loud smack on her cheek.

Sadie turned to Mad Dog. "And you must be Mad Dog. The guys have been talking about you non-stop since they got back from Colorado." She held out her hand to him.

When he reached out to take it, the baby leaned sharply forward.

Sadie dove to catch her, but Mad Dog scooped her up before she fell from her mother's arms.

Sadie laughed. "I think someone wants to get to know you." She held out her arms. "If you want me to take her, I can. She has a habit of spitting up on people when you least expect it."

"I can handle a little spit," Mad Dog said and blew a raspberry on the child's chubby belly. "Hey, Emma. Who's your favorite uncle?"

Jolie smiled. This was a side of Mad Dog she hadn't seen. Though the man had been raised by an uncaring father, he was a natural with the little girl. He'd be great with children of his own.

Inside her belly, she suddenly felt a hollowness. She'd always imagined raising her own children on the ranch where she'd grown up. She'd pictured her father teaching them how to ride and shoot and rope steers.

She swallowed hard at the lump forming in her throat. Her father wouldn't be the one to teach her children anything. And her job would preclude her from ever having children. What woman would risk having children when she could be the target of a terrorist at any given moment?

Three men emerged from the house and descended the steps to surround Sadie, Emma, Jolie and Mad Dog.

A tall man with brown hair and green eyes clapped his hand on Mad Dog's back. "Mad Dog, you old son-of-a-bi—"

Sadie touched his arm. "Hank..."

"Sorry." The man grimaced, and then grinned. "You look better than the last time I saw you." He touched his own chin. "Glad you scraped the wool off your face. You don't look like something the cat dragged in."

Mad Dog's lips twisted in a wry grin. "Thanks, I think."

Hank touched the baby in Mad Dog's arms. "I see you've met my girls."

"I have." Mad Dog held Emma, smiling. "You are going to have your hands full with this one. Wait until she's a teen."

Emma leaned toward her father and giggled.

Hank took her, tossed her into the air, caught her and kissed her cheek. "I have a special shotgun for that time and a team of Spec Ops guys I can deploy on surveillance missions."

Mad Dog laughed. "I know you'd do it, too." He turned to Jolie. "Hank, this is Jolie Richards. Jolie, this is my old commander, Hank Patterson."

"Not so old. Still young enough to kick Mad Dog's ass—"

Again, Sadie touched Hank's arm.

Hank sighed. "It takes some getting used to, having to watch my language around Emma." He handed the baby to Sadie and held out a hand to Jolie. "Glad to finally meet you. I've heard good things through the grapevine."

Jolie gripped the man's hand, but instead of shaking it, Hank pulled her into a bear hug. "We'll do whatever it takes to help you." He stepped back and waved to the other two men. "Guys, this is Jolie. Jolie…" He pointed to the first man, a brute of a guy with brown hair and brown eyes. "This is Bear, a former Delta Force soldier. His fiancée is a good friend of Sadie's."

Bear nodded and extended his hand.

Jolie shook it, amazed at the power behind the grip. "Nice to meet you."

"And this is Kujo," Hank continued, waving the other guy forward. That's when she noticed the German Shepherd at his heels.

"Pleasure," Kujo said and shook her hand. "My partner is Six."

"Six?" Jolie questioned.

"It's a long story," Kujo said. "The short version is that he was the sixth MWD—military working dog—"

"Will he take my arm off if I pet him?"

Kujo laughed. "No. His specialty was bomb-sniffing. But he can take a man down if given the right command." He nodded toward the dog. "Go ahead."

Jolie reached out a hand, her fingers curled under in case the dog decided they looked like a threat or food.

Six sniffed her hand but didn't bite.

Emboldened, Jolie slipped her hand along the dog's jaw and up to his ears where she gave him a good scratch.

Six leaned into her hand, closing his eyes as if in heaven.

Jolie chuckled. "He's beautiful."

"Could have used him this morning," Mad Dog said.

Hank frowned. "What happened?"

"Can we take the conversation inside?" Sadie said. "It's a little cool to have Emma out much longer."

Hank held the door for the group to enter the house.

Sadie led them into a massive living area with cathedral ceilings and giant picture windows overlooking the Crazy Mountains.

"I'll get drinks. Everyone up for lemonade? It's too early for beer."

"It's never too early for beer," Bear said. "But lemonade sounds great. Thanks, Sadie."

Sadie disappeared with Emma.

Jolie and Mad Dog spent the next fifteen minutes giving Hank the rundown of all that had happened in the past twenty-four hours.

"You really could have used Six this morning," Kujo commented. "He might have saved you a truck."

"He might have saved more than that, if Jolie hadn't had the wherewithal to get us the hell out before the bomb detonated."

Sadie returned with a tray filled with a pitcher and six glasses. "Emma's down for a nap." She poured a round of drinks for everyone and perched on the arm of a leather chair. "Sounds like you need more protection."

Hank paced the floor head down, his lips pressed into a thin line. "Lambert said you were to work autonomously in your efforts to find this Nadir dude, and I understand his motives. Nadir might not make a move if he thought Miss Richards was surrounded by a team of trained operatives. She has to appear unguarded and unprotected for him to feel like he can come out of hiding to take her down." Hank stopped pacing and looked up. "It would defeat the purpose of luring him to Montana."

"Exactly," Jolie said.

"So, how do you explain your presence with Miss Richards?" Hank asked.

Jolie's cheeks heated.

Mad Dog glanced at her, and then back to Hank. "I'm undercover as Jolie's fiancé."

Bear, Kujo and Sadie all grinned.

"Perfect," Hank said. "No one would question that you're sticking close to her. Newly engaged couples tend to be all over each other." His lips quirked upward on the corners. "Right, Sadie?"

She smiled. "We were."

"How can we assist if we can't get close?" Bear asked.

"We get close enough and wait for a call for help," Hank said.

"Except, we don't have a land line out at the house, and we don't get cell phone coverage."

Hank nodded. "I have a solution for that. Follow me." He led the way to a door with a specialized keypad, similar to the ones used at CIA headquarters.

He entered a code and pressed his thumb to a reader. A loud click could be heard. Hank gripped the door handle and opened the door.

Stairs led into a darkened basement.

Jolie followed Hank, and the other three men descended after her.

As Hank neared the bottom of the staircase, motion-sensor lights blinked on, illuminating a large room.

A big man with blond hair and blue eyes sat in the corner, staring at a computer. He looked up and blinked. "Wow, I didn't realize the lights went out until they came back on."

"Jolie, Mad Dog, this is Swede, former Navy SEAL and current computer guru. When he's not out chasing bad guys or guarding celebrities, he's hacking into systems all over the world."

"Mad Dog." Swede nodded. "Heard about you from Hank. Just sorry we didn't cross paths on active duty." He rose, stretched and crossed the room to shake hands with Jolie, and then Mad Dog. "Hank told me what you're up against. I've been surfing the net, looking for chatter. Think I found some."

"Yeah?" Mad Dog shook the man's hand. "Like what?"

"Heavy recruiting, tapping into the locals in this area."

Jolie's gut twisted. She glanced at Mad Dog.

He was looking at her.

"Could you trace the chatter to an IP address?" Hank asked.

Swede held up a sticky note. "Better than that, I traced to an IP address, and from there, a physical address."

Mad Dog took the paper and handed it to Jolie. "Recognize the address?"

She read it and shook her head. "Not off the top of my head. I know the general direction but not who lives there."

Hank turned to Swede. "Have Taz and Boomer check it out."

"We should go with them," Bear offered.

"If possible, I'd rather they sneak in and out without being seen," Hank said. "I want these people to continue their chatter. We might learn more from them, if they think we aren't on to them."

"Should we send Six with them?" Kujo stepped up. "If this gang is involved, they might have booby-trapped this location like they did the cave."

"No. Six needs to go with Mad Dog and Agent Richards in case her house has been rigged with explosives. We'll let Taz and Boomer know to be on the lookout for tripwires."

"Taking Six is an offer we can't afford to pass up," Mad Dog said. "You'll have to give me a crash course in the commands."

"And Six will have to familiarize with you on those commands," Kujo said. "It took me a while to calm him down after his last deployment. He suffered PTSD from too much time in theater. We need to get him used to answering your commands. He doesn't answer to just anyone."

"Right," Mad Dog said. "I'll do whatever it takes to keep Jolie from being blown up in another IED explosion."

"You said you didn't have a land line or cell phone coverage at your place." Hank opened a cabinet and pulled out a satellite phone. "Take this. It should be able to pick up a signal just about anywhere." He checked the battery, and then handed it to Mad Dog. "And you might need more firepower." He opened another door and led them deeper into the basement.

The light blinked on, shining onto racks of rifles, shotguns and military-grade weaponry. "If you need it, take it. That's why we have such an extensive armory."

"Expecting World War III?" Mad Dog asked.

Hank laughed. "No, but we're ready for a riot or a

takeover. I want my team to have whatever they need to get the job done, no matter how big or small." He looked to Mad Dog then to Jolie. "That being said, if either of you needs anything…"

"I have all the weaponry I need," Jolie said.

"I could use a rifle and three dozen rounds," Mad Dog said, "as well as nine-millimeter rounds."

Hank selected an AR15 rifle with a scope and loaded several boxes of cartridges into a bag. "Communications equipment?"

"Two-way radios for me and Jolie," Mad Dog said, his voice clipped.

"Done." Two tiny radio headsets were loaded into the bag.

"GPS tracking chip for Jolie and a tracker for me."

"I refuse to be microchipped like a dog," Jolie muttered.

Hank grinned. "I have something better." He reached into a drawer and pulled out a necklace with a pretty ruby-colored stone. "Do you wear jewelry, Agent Richards?" he asked.

She shook her head.

"Start now. Not only is it pretty, it has a tracking chip embedded in the stone's setting. My wife wears one, and I'm getting them for all my men to give to their significant others. We hope we never have to use them, but if we do, we'll be a lot faster finding you than without it."

"I'll wear it." Jolie wasn't sure she liked being tracked, but given the current situation, she figured it would be smart to give her protectors a clue as to where to find her should Nadir manage to capture her.

Jolie and Mad Dog spent the next hour with Kujo and Six, familiarizing with the dog and the commands they might need to deploy the animal. By the time they finished, Sadie and Hank had lunch on the table in the dining room.

The men spent the meal sharing stories about their years on active duty.

Jolie could relate to some of their exploits, but not to the dust and grit in their hair and eyes. She'd never been to the Middle East. Most of her assignments had been in Europe and Russia.

Though some of the men hadn't served with the others, they shared a strong bond of brotherhood.

Sadie leaned over and whispered in her ear, "They're pretty amazing, aren't they?"

Jolie nodded. "They've sacrificed so much."

"And so have you. It can't be easy for a woman in a mostly man's field, doing what you do."

Jolie nodded. She'd been in tight situations where her abilities to blend into the woodwork and escape quickly had been the only reasons she was still alive.

But she'd worked very much on her own, not in a team, like the SEALs and Delta Force guys had. They had people to depend on and who depended on them to get them through the rough spots.

Jolie realized she was glad Mad Dog had come along when he had. Facing her old home was hard enough, without having to deal with a terrorist on her trail. She might not admit it to Mad Dog, but she was glad he had her six.

All too soon, lunch was over and it was time to head back to the Rocking R Ranch. If the chatter on the internet was any indication, Nadir knew where she was and had enlisted people to help him in the effort to take her out.

She might as well get back, dig in and be ready before nightfall. If anything was going to happen, it would probably happen that night. The box of condoms would have to wait.

CHAPTER 12

MAD DOG DROVE BACK to town with Jolie in the passenger seat and Six in the rear of the vehicle, lying patiently on the carpet. Knowing he had a bomb-sniffing dog made him feel a little better about staying in Jolie's house that night.

Hank had promised to have Swede and Kujo nearby, without being too close, in case they needed backup. They would be a satellite phone call away.

Once they reached Eagle Rock, Jolie's cell phone beeped.

She dug in her back pocket and pulled it out. "Who would be texting me? I don't give out my number to just anyone." She read the message and her face paled. "What the hell?"

"What does it say?"

"It's a warning."

Mad Dog pulled the SUV over on the side of the

road, scanning the buildings around them and the rooftops for any potential threat. "From who?"

Jolie shook her head. "Caller ID is blocked. I don't know."

"What exactly does it say?" he asked.

"Leave Montana, or else." She glanced up at Mad Dog, and then back at the phone. She typed with her thumbs, talking as she did. "Or else what?" After she hit send, she waited for a reply, but none came.

Mad Dog had the satellite phone out and was hitting the numbers to connect with Hank.

"Already in trouble?" Hank's voice came across on the first ring.

"Jolie got a text on her cell phone here in town. Blocked caller. Can Swede trace that text?"

"If not, we have connections with people who could."

Mad Dog handed the sat phone to Jolie. She gave Hank her phone number and told him what the message said.

"Cryptic."

"Yes, but who would have my number? I don't give it out."

"I'll have my people look at it and get back to you as soon as they know anything."

"Thank you."

"Jolie, is Mad Dog close?" Hank asked. "He needs to hear this as well."

Jolie leaned across the console and held the satellite phone where she and Mad Dog could hear at the same time.

"We're both here, sir," she said.

"The IP address we talked about earlier belongs to a Mr. Ty Kingston. Name sound familiar?"

Her eyebrows drew together. "Sounds familiar, but I don't remember him. I've been gone eight years."

"He was an older gentleman. Your father might have known him. It appears he died six months ago, but his place still has electricity and a satellite dish. No one bothered to shut it off. Taz and Boomer checked it out. They didn't find anyone there at the time, but the place is tucked back in the woods away from the road. Unless someone was going there, no one would suspect it was still occupied."

Jolie gave Mad Dog a charged glance. "Someone has to be paying the bills, or the services would have been cut off."

"Swede learned from the friendly lady at the electric company that the bills have been paid for with money orders. It'll take longer to trace the source of the money orders. We suspect the satellite internet service was funded in the same way. I'll let you know if we learn anything else on that, and on the blocked caller. In the meantime, watch your back, and call us at the first sign of trouble."

"Yes, sir." Mad Dog ended the call and shifted into DRIVE. "Are you sure you want to go back to your house?"

Jolie sat, staring straight ahead. "I came out here to bait a terrorist. I don't plan on leaving without accomplishing my mission."

Mad Dog chuckled, though he didn't think her

words were funny. "I thought that would be your response. Let's go catch Nadir."

Flashing lights ahead of them made Mad Dog pause before pulling onto the road.

Sheriff Barron pulled up beside him, got out of his patrol car and stepped up to Mad Dog's window.

Mad Dog lowered the glass.

"I'm glad I caught you two. I just got back from your ranch after spending a couple hours there with the state crime lab folks." He shook his head. "You two are lucky to be alive. Your truck is a complete loss."

Mad Dog already knew that. "They find anything that would link the bombing to anyone?"

"Not yet, but they loaded your truck onto a flatbed and hauled it off to their lab. Which could be days, if not weeks, before they untangle that mess."

Jolie leaned across the console. "Is it clear for us to return to the house?"

"You can go home," the sheriff said. "But I suggest you stay in town. Whoever did that is playing for keeps."

"Thank you, Sheriff, but I prefer to sleep in my own bed." Jolie opened her jacket. "We're armed, and we have a bomb-sniffing dog. Hopefully, we won't be caught unaware again."

The sheriff drew in a deep breath and let it out. "Okay, then, I'll have one of my men swing by later tonight. Don't shoot him." The man straightened and turned toward his vehicle.

"Sheriff Barron." Jolie's voice stopped him.

He turned and bent to see her through the window. "Yes, ma'am."

"Don't send one of your men. If anything happens out there, I'd rather your guys weren't caught in the crossfire."

Sheriff Barron frowned. "Jolie, that's what we're here for."

"You're here for the good people of Eagle Rock. Not for people like me who've purposely brought trouble home." She grimaced. "I wish, now, that I hadn't. So please, don't send your men by. I'd hate it if one of them was hurt because of what I've done."

The sheriff's frown deepened. "Jolie, I've known you since you were a little girl. You are one of the good people of Eagle Rock. You deserve our protection as much as anyone. But if you don't want us out there, I can't force you to go along with my wishes." He touched a finger to his cowboy hat. "Take care of yourself. I'd like to see you stay here and make it your home again."

"Thank you, Sheriff." Jolie sat back in her seat and stared at the road ahead. "Take me home, Caleb."

Mad Dog complied. They had a job to do. Though he wanted to wrap her up in an ironclad safety net, he couldn't. She was a CIA agent. He was there to protect her, but more importantly, he was there to eradicate the threat.

JOLIE'S GUT told her Nadir was near, and that he would make his move soon. If not himself, then with his recruits. She had to be ready for either event.

So intent on getting home and setting up her defenses, she missed the flash in the side mirror.

"Hold on," Mad Dog said. "We have company." He jammed his foot on the accelerator, and the SUV shot forward, speeding through the twists and turns of the mountain road.

Just as Jolie turned to see what was behind them, an old truck slammed into the SUV's left rear bumper sending them spinning sideways into a curve with a steep drop-off on one side.

Jolie gripped the armrest, tempted to close her eyes. Morbid curiosity kept them wide open.

Mad Dog fought the steering wheel, pumped the brakes and struggled to keep the SUV from flying off the side of the mountain.

Just as the tires grabbed the road and Mad Dog straightened the vehicle, the truck hit them again.

Jolie had turned in time to see the driver and gasped. She didn't have time to shout out who their attacker was, because he pushed the SUV off the road, and it plummeted down the hillside.

"Hold on!" Mad Dog yelled. He steered as best he could over the rocks and around trees and boulders.

The seatbelt held Jolie tight against the seat as they bounced and jolted until the ground leveled out onto an old logging road.

Mad Dog brought the SUV to a halt and reached over to capture Jolie's hand. "Are you okay?"

She nodded, her head still rattled from the wild ride down the steep embankment. Her first thought was for Six. She turned at the same time as Mad Dog to find the dog on the floorboard, shaking.

Six hopped up onto the seat and stared out the window, seemingly uninjured.

Jolie pressed her other hand to her chest and laughed. "I can't believe we survived that."

He snorted. "Or that this SUV is still running."

She clutched his fingers in hers. "I saw the driver."

"You did?" Mad Dog glanced back up the hill. "Who was it?"

Jolie followed his gaze, but couldn't see the road above through the trees and brush. Thankfully, the man who'd pushed them off the road wouldn't be able to see them.

"Brandon Lewis."

Mad Dog shook his head. "The Lewis's teenaged son?"

She nodded.

"Why would he do that?"

"I have no idea. I can't think of anything you or I could have done to make him mad enough to want to kill us."

"Unless he's one of Nadir's 'soldiers'." Mad Dog shifted the SUV into DRIVE and followed the road. "Any idea where this comes out?"

Jolie shook her head. "None. Most logging roads eventually come out on a highway."

Mad Dog glanced around the cab. "Where'd that satellite phone go?"

Jolie searched the cab and found it under the seat.

"Call Hank and let him know what you saw."

"Where are we headed?" she asked.

"I'd go to the Lewis's, but I think we need time to set

up our defenses at your place. I believe tonight will be the night Nadir makes his move."

Jolie nodded. Deep inside, she had the same feeling. She punched the number for Hank and waited.

"I was just about to call you two," Hank answered without preamble.

"Why?" she asked.

"Found out who the blocked call was from."

"Would that blocked call have come from Brandon Lewis?" she questioned, looking over at Mad Dog as she did.

"Yes, it was. How did you know?" Hank asked.

"He just ran us off the road." Jolie explained the situation ending with, "We're headed to the Rocking R Ranch."

"You don't want to question Brandon's parents?"

"Not now. We need time to set up defenses before dusk," Jolie said. "We think Nadir will make his move tonight."

"I'll send a couple of my guys out to watch the Lewis's place. That will put them close enough to get to you quickly. Don't worry. I'll tell them to keep a low profile and report, rather than engage."

"Thank you, Hank," Jolie said. "Out here." She ended the call and stared across the console at Mad Dog, shaking inside—from tension, not fear. This was really happening. "You don't have to stay through this."

His lips tightened. "Yes, I do."

But Jolie didn't want to see him hurt. "This was my operation. I can deal with the repercussions."

"You forget, I was assigned to be your partner. I

leave no man...or woman...behind." He winked at her. "Besides, you've saved my life a couple of times. I owe you."

"You don't owe me anything," she said.

He slowed the SUV before the dirt road ended and brought the vehicle to a stop. "Jolie, you need to understand. You saved me before we even met. I was on the edge of a cliff, contemplating my worth in this life, when Hank showed up and hooked me up with my new boss. If you hadn't needed help, I might not be here today."

Her gaze met his, and she frowned. "You were considering..."

He nodded. "The bottom of that cliff looked a lot easier to deal with than a life with no purpose." Mad Dog brought her hand to his lips. "Even if what we have between us goes nowhere, you've shown me that I have a lot more life to live. A purposeful life. And I don't have to do it alone."

How many times had she'd felt so very alone in this world? She'd been on the edge of a cliff many times—if not physically, then mentally. With no family back home, no one to call when she was feeling down and no one to talk to on a lonely night, she'd been where Mad Dog had been that day on the cliff. Her eyes stung with unshed tears. "How did I show you that? I haven't made a commitment to you. Nor have you made one to me."

"Your strength and determination to make things right in this world forced me to see how deep I'd sunk into my own funk. You made me realize the world does not revolve around me. I could still use my skills for good. If not with the organization I'm a part of now, then somewhere else. Maybe a deputy, a firefighter or an EMT. I can help others and, by so doing, help myself. Don't you see? By just being you, you saved me."

Jolie leaned across the console and pressed a finger to his lips. "Did anyone ever tell you that you talk too much?" Then she wrapped her hand around the back of his neck and pulled him close to brush her lips across his.

He cupped her face in his palms and deepened the connection, his tongue thrusting past her teeth to caress hers.

When they finally surfaced for air, Jolie laughed.

Six barked in the back of the vehicle, reminding them he was still alive and well.

Mad Dog chuckled and soon joined in with Jolie's laughter.

Jolie wiped tears from her eyes and touched his cheek. "You realize we were almost killed, and we have a shit-load of preparations to make before we face Nadir and his ghouls?"

"I do." Mad Dog grinned. "But for some reason, I can't wipe the smile off my face. I've never felt more alive and in tune with the world than at this moment."

"Me, either." She took his hand in hers and kissed his palm. "Don't think you owe me a life for yours. You came to me at just the right time. I needed you here more than you can ever know."

"We make a good team."

"Yes, we do." She pressed his palm to her cheek, and then released it. "Let's go get us a terrorist."

CHAPTER 13

MAD DOG SURVEYED the exterior of Jolie's home.

Six had done his job and sniffed around the house for any explosive devices. The only spot he'd sat next to was the burn scar on the ground where the truck had been. The house was clear.

Mad Dog kept Six outside with him for the afternoon, figuring the dog might alert him to anyone who might try to sneak up on him while he was working.

They'd used old lumber they'd found in the barn to board up the windows, leaving enough room for clear lines of fire. With only two of them, they'd be hard-pressed to cover all sides of the house. He wasn't even sure they should be in the house when the shit hit the fan.

They might be better off hunkered down in the tree line. But they had no idea when Nadir would stage his attack, or how many people would be involved. For all they knew, he might come alone. In which case, he'd sneak up on them, and they wouldn't know from which direction.

Hell, he could be watching them as they worked that afternoon. That's why Mad Dog had Jolie work inside the house. No use making her a target by having her outside.

At Jolie's suggestion, Mad Dog had turned the horses out into the pasture and shooed them away from the barn. If bullets started flying, she didn't want the horses to take a hit for her. Neither did Mad Dog. They didn't deserve to be caught in the crossfire.

The sun dropped below the mountain tops, taking the landscape from daylight to dusk in less than thirty minutes.

Jolie had a pot of chili cooking on the stove, the scent finding its way through the screen door to the front porch where Mad Dog was hammering the last nail into a board covering the big picture windows.

He turned to study the landscape, tree line and the road leading up to the house. Nothing moved in the shadowy gray light. Not even the crickets and cicadas had begun their nightly song.

He felt as if time had suspended, waiting for some-thing to happen. His muscles were tense, just like they'd been before every mission into the Afghan hills or an Iraqi town.

Six whimpered, as if sensing Mad Dog's disquiet.

Together, they dropped down off the porch, circled the barn and the house once more, before entering through the back door into the kitchen.

Jolie had two bowls in her hands, carrying them to

the table. "Have a seat. We might as well fuel up." She pointed to the bowl of dog food on the floor by the back door and gave Six the command to eat.

The dog sniffed at the bowl then dug in.

Mad Dog waited until Jolie took her seat before seating himself. Then he leaned over the bowl, inhaling deeply. "I didn't know you could cook."

"I don't advertise the fact. My father and I had our specialties. Mine was chili and lasagna; his was grilled steaks, roasted chicken and mashed potatoes. We learned enough to survive and took turns."

"I learned how to make mac-n-cheese and ramen noodles to survive when my father drank the grocery money."

Jolie reached for his hand across the table. "I'm sorry. You must have had it rough."

"Don't be sorry," he said. "I learned a lot about self-preservation. It helped me during SEAL BUD/S training." He grinned. "Since then, a friend of mine taught me how to make chicken enchiladas and Mexican cornbread." His smile faded. Frito and his wife had been good friends. He made a note to himself to check on Rosa and the baby once they got past this assignment.

"I love Mexican food," Jolie exclaimed. "Will you make enchiladas for me someday?"

He winked. "You're on." Mad Dog liked the idea that they would be together long enough for him to cook a meal for her. Perhaps, he'd been shortsighted by not investing in a box of condoms. If tonight really was the night they bagged the terrorist, his job here would be done, the danger to Jolie would be over and they could get on with their lives.

Which also meant leaving Montana. He'd go on to his next assignment as a Sleeper SEAL and Jolie would move on to her next assignment as a CIA agent.

As he finished his bowl of chili, Mad Dog looked around the kitchen of the ranch house. It needed to be remodeled and upgraded, but it seemed homey. He could almost feel the love Jolie and her father had shared in that kitchen. It would be a great home in which to raise children.

"Are you sure you'll sell this place once this assignment is over?" he asked. He concentrated on the chili, but, in his peripheral vision, he could see Jolie's expression change from happy to sad.

"I have to admit, being back has been an emotional roller coaster. When I first got here, all I could think about was getting a For Sale sign up as soon as possible. I didn't want the bad memories to haunt me the rest of my life."

"And now?" He looked up.

She set her spoon on the table beside her empty bowl and gave him half a smile. "Now, all I can remember is the happiness of growing up here. I see my mother in the furniture, knick-knacks, pictures on the walls and the quilts on the beds. The memories of my father are strong in the kitchen, the living room, the barn and the pastures. Everywhere I look, I feel him around me."

"It'll be hard to let go," he said quietly.

She sighed and shook her head. "What use do I have

for a ranch in Montana? If I go back to my job, I'm based out of Virginia. I could be sent anywhere in the world. I can't manage a ranch like that. This place has fallen into disrepair. It needs a family to run it and live in this house. It's not right for me to keep it when I won't be here. The only way I would keep it is if I quit my job."

He held still. "Have you considered it?"

"I hadn't, until I came home..." Her lips twisted into a wry grin. "I still call it home. I haven't lived anywhere else I ever thought of as my home...that place you come back to."

"My active duty friends with wives always say home is where the heart is," Mad Dog said. "No matter where they move, home is where their wives and kids are."

"For me, it's where my memories are. I don't have family here. They're gone."

"But they live on." Mad Dog nodded toward the kitchen. "In the house, in the barn. Everywhere."

Jolie shook her head and touched her hand to her chest. "No. They live here. But they're just memories. I need to get on with my life. I can't live in the past. Memories don't keep you warm at night."

Mad Dog stood and took her hand in his. "No, but people do." He pulled her into his arms and held her close. There was nothing sexual in the way he hugged her. Just one human being connecting with another. "You don't get this from a memory."

She wrapped her arms around his waist and laid her cheek against his chest. "No, you don't."

"You deserve to have a life filled with love and

happiness, Jolie. Don't give up on it because you lost your father and mother."

Her arms tightened around him. "What about you? You've sacrificed so much for this country. You deserve to love and be loved. You can't stand on the edge of a cliff wondering what's left in life."

He chuckled. "We are a pair, aren't we?"

"Two lonely souls in a boarded-up house in the backwoods of Montana."

"What are the chances of finding what we're looking for here?" he whispered against her hair.

"I don't know. Some would say it's too soon. We haven't known each other long enough."

"Sounds strange," Mad Dog said, raising his hands to cup the back of her head and tipping her face upward. "But I feel like I've known you all my life. Like you've always been a part of me. I just had to find you."

She smiled up at him. "Not strange at all. I feel the same." Then she rose on her toes and pressed her lips to his.

The warm, platonic hug morphed into something completely different.

Mad Dog couldn't get enough of her lips, her mouth...her heart. He wanted to be closer than body to body. He wanted more from one person than he'd ever imagined possible.

Jolie threaded her fingers into his hair in a frenetic dance, digging into his scalp, her mouth pressing hard against his.

The satellite phone rang several times before the sound broke through the lusty haze clouding Mad Dog's judgment. He drew back. "We have to stop this before we get stupid and forget why we're here."

She nodded and rubbed the back of her hand over swollen lips. "Right." Then she came up on her toes again, kissed him lightly and backed away. "We have a job to do. And that's the satellite phone ringing."

They spent a minute or two searching the house for where they'd laid it, finding it on an end table in the living room.

"Mad Dog, what's your status?"

"So far, everything's quiet."

"Got news from my surveillance team at the Lewis house."

"Go ahead."

"The teen hasn't returned home," Hank said. "The only one there at this time is Mr. Lewis." I have a man in town, keeping an eye out for Brandon and listening for any rumblings about any events going down."

"Good to know. If he tried to kill us once, he might be in with Nadir and come after us again."

"Keep your heads down. All you need do is call if things even hint at getting hot tonight."

"Will do." Mad Dog ended the call.

"Looks like we might have more than just Nadir to deal with tonight." Jolie drew in a deep breath and let it out. "Let's get in place. I'll take the front of the house."

Mad Dog didn't argue. Jolie was the better shot. He grabbed the bag of equipment Hank had sent home with them and rummaged through, grinning when he found night vision goggles.

"Take these." He handed a pair to Jolie along with a

radio headset. "I'll walk into the living room, so we can test the communications."

He slipped the headset on and flicked the switch to activate it. Then he settled the other set over Jolie's ears and switched hers on before walking around the corner into the living room.

Six followed him and paced the length of the room and back.

"Hey, good-looking," Jolie's gravely female voice sounded in Mad Dog's ear. "Wanna have fun tonight?"

"I think we're going to have more fun than we can handle." The communication devices worked fine. A glance through the cracks in the boarded windows showed dusk had turned to dark. Night had settled in on the mountain ranch.

Now, all they had to do was wait.

THE ROAR of engines sounded nearby.

Six growled low in his throat.

Suddenly, out of the tree line burst half a dozen or more motorcycles, their headlights shining onto the front of the house.

"Break's over," Mad Dog said into the mic. "We have company. I'll take the front, since I'm here."

"Manning the back."

"Place that call to Hank, Sweetheart. Nadir pulled out all the stops and called in his minions. We're already outnumbered."

JOLIE HATED that she wasn't in the front of the house to see what was going on. But she could hear the engines roaring as the motorcycles poured into the yard. She fumbled with the satellite phone, finally hitting the numbers for Hank.

He answered on the first ring. "Tell me."

"The motorcycle gang is back."

"Any sign of Nadir?"

"Can't tell. But we're outnumbered."

"Sending in the cavalry. Hang tight."

"Incoming!" Mad Dog said into her ear. "Molotov cocktail just landed on the front porch. They're going to burn the place down. Get out the back door. Now!"

"Looks like we're going to abandon the house," Jolie said. "They're playing with fire."

"We'll be there as quickly as possible. Take cover somewhere safe."

"Roger. Out." Jolie ended the call, grabbed her rifle and the fire extinguisher her father had kept hanging on the wall by the backdoor. It was old, but it was the only one they had. She prayed it still worked, or the house would burn to the ground. Armed with her rifle and the extinguisher, she ran to the front of the house.

"What are you doing?" Mad Dog yelled. "You have to get out now. Go through the back door. Now. I'll cover while you run for the tree line."

"I can't leave you here."

"You have to." He kissed her quickly. "I'll be fine. Now go."

She shoved the extinguisher into his hands. "Not sure this'll work, but it's worth a shot."

"Thanks." He touched his finger to his headset. "Tell me when you're safe."

She nodded and headed for the back door.

By the time she reached it, she heard footsteps on the porch outside. She couldn't get out that way. Her only other choices were going through a window, which all led out onto the porch where the bad guys were, or to go through the basement window.

She'd crawled out that portal many times, playing hide and seek as a child. It led out the north side of the house into a stand of bushes that would conceal her exit until she was able to make a run for the tree line.

Jolie ran through the basement door, closed it behind her, descended the stairs and hurried to the window at the far end. Not until she reached it did she remember Mad Dog had nailed boards over it to keep the raccoon out.

She grabbed a pry bar from her father's tools and ripped the boards off the window frame, opened the broken window and climbed up onto the boxes stacked beneath. First, she lowered her rifle onto the ground, careful not to damage the scope. Then she pulled herself through the opening and out into the night.

Once outside, the motorcycle noise was deafening. Lights shone like strobes as the bike riders circled the front yard and around the back of the house, crossing in front of the bushes behind which Jolie hid.

In between the bikers' passes, Jolie, with her rifle in one hand, low-crawled to the edge of the bushes, parted the branches and waited for her chance to make a run for the tree line.

A biker roared past. And then nothing.

Bunching her legs beneath her, she launched out of the bushes and ran for the trees.

At that moment, another bike raced around the corner.

Jolie didn't have time to pull out her handgun or bring her rifle to her shoulder before the rider was on her, grabbed her around the middle and flung her across his legs. He lost control of the handlebars, and the bike tipped over, skidding to a halt in the dust.

Jolie slammed her hand into the Adam's apple of the man who'd grabbed her. While her attacker clutched at his throat struggling to breathe, Jolie rolled off him and the bike, scrambled to her feet and got her bearings. She'd lost her rifle in the tumble, and it was too dark to search for it. Knowing she only had seconds before others discovered her, she ran for the trees again.

She hadn't gone ten yards when another biker spun around the side of the house, ditched his bike in front of her and tackled her to the ground, knocking her headset off in the process.

"I can't catch a freakin' break!" she muttered, balled her fist and cocked her arm, ready to punch the guy in the throat when a female voice behind her said.

"Don't do it, or I'll shoot your boyfriend."

Jolie's arm froze.

The young man who'd tackled her jumped to his feet. He'd lost his helmet in the fall off the motorcycle, his face now visible in the light from the quarter moon just rising over the ridge.

"Brandon?" she exclaimed.

He didn't look happy, and his arm was bleeding where he'd torn his jacket in the crash.

"You shouldn't have come back," he said.

"But this is my property."

His gaze shifted from her face to over her shoulder.

Jolie turned to the woman standing behind her. She wore black jeans, a black jacket and boots, and she held a pistol pointed at Jolie's chest. "Sherry?"

The other woman's lips pressed into a thin line. "You shouldn't have come back," she said. "Everything would have been fine if you had stayed the hell gone."

Jolie shook her head. "I don't understand. Our families have known each other forever. You were friends with my father. Why would you join a gang?"

She snorted. "I'm not part of this gang. I'm only here to protect my son."

"Mother," Brandon held up his hand. "Don't do this."

"I won't have you going to jail. You didn't do anything wrong."

"I know it was an accident," he said, his voice hoarse, "but I should have told someone."

"You were already on probation. They would have sent you to jail."

"For what?" Jolie asked.

"For killing your father," Brandon blurted out. Tears welled in the young man's eyes. "I didn't do it on purpose. I thought he was a deer. I shot him, because I thought he was a deer. Now you know. I can't give you back your father, but now you know why he died."

"It's okay, Brandon," his mother said. "We'll make this all right. No one else has to know." Her face hardened in the moonlight. "And no one will, once we take care of her."

"No mother. You can't do this. I can't live like this anymore." Brandon walked toward his mother. "If you want to shoot her, you'll have to shoot me. I won't be a part of this."

Jolie braced for her getaway. As she swung around to run, an arm clamped around her middle trapping her arms beneath it.

"It's too late," a deep male voice said against her ear. "You're already a part of this." His free arm rose with a pistol, and he fired, hitting Sherry in the chest.

Sherry dropped her weapon, clutched at the wound with one hand and reached toward her son with the other. "Son," she said, blood oozing from her mouth. Then she fell to the earth.

Jolie's captor flung her way from him and into Brandon. "Hold her."

Still in shock, Brandon grabbed Jolie.

She could have fought him, but she didn't have anywhere to go. Surrounded by the gang and targeted by Nadir, she was doomed. And all she could think about was Mad Dog. Where was he? She thought she'd heard gunfire. Had they gotten to him? She couldn't give up until she knew he was okay.

By now, other bikers surrounded them, shining their headlights at Jolie, Brandon and Nadir.

"Kill her," Nadir said. "Take your knife and cut her throat."

"Don't listen to him, Brandon," Jolie whispered. "My father's death was an accident."

"I'm sorry," he said. "I should have told someone else besides my mother. Now, she's...she's..."

"Your mother is dead because of you," Nadir said. "She shouldn't have come."

"No, Brandon, she's dead because of Nadir," Jolie said. "You didn't kill her—he did."

"This woman is a murderer. She kills people for a living. She killed my brother," Nadir raised his voice, his tone intense and somehow hypnotic. "She'll kill you, and then she will go after your father."

Brandon's hand tightened on her. "Leave my father out of this. He's done nothing to hurt anyone."

"I know that, Brandon. Nadir is using you. Don't listen to him."

"Shut up, woman! Shut up!" Nadir, his face red with anger, fired into the air. "Kill her, now! Or I'll kill you."

The bikers gathered around chanted, "Kill her! Kill her! Kill her!"

Brandon pulled a knife from the scabbard on his belt and pressed the cold metal blade to her throat.

Jolie tensed, knowing that if she broke away now, Nadir or one of the others would put a bullet into her. But she couldn't go down without a fight. She wouldn't.

CHAPTER 14

MAD DOG HAD POSITIONED the fire extinguisher at the gap in the window he was supposed to be using to fire his rifle through. But he couldn't see anything past the flames rising from the fuel that had exploded on impact from the Molotov cocktail. He poked the hose through the window, held his breath and prayed the eight-year-old extinguisher would work after all these years.

He pulled the handle and white powder blasted toward the fuel, extinguishing the flames. By then the bikers were circling the house, blasting through the yard, stirring up dust.

He hadn't heard from Jolie since she'd promised to let him know when she'd made it to safety, and he was worried.

Then the bikers disappeared around the side of the house, deserting the front yard.

Something was happening, and it couldn't be good. Mad Dog suspected Jolie was in trouble. He called to

Six and ran toward the kitchen, the last place he knew she'd been.

The satellite phone lay on the table. He hit the numbers for Hank and waited precious seconds for him to answer on the first ring.

"Jolie?" Hank answered.

"No, it's Mad Dog. We need backup."

"Swede and Boomer should be there by now. I'm with Bear and Taz, we're inbound. ETA five mikes."

"That might be too late. I think they have Jolie. I'm headed out to find out."

"Wait for backup."

"I can't. It might be too late. If we don't make it, be sure to get Nadir. The man can't be allowed to continue." He didn't wait for Hank's response. Instead, he tossed the phone on the table and slipped through the back door with Six.

Outside he heard chanting from the side of the house he couldn't see. He left the porch and, hugging the bushes, hurried toward the sound. As the words became clear, his heart dropped to the pit of his belly.

"Kill her! Kill her!"

The situation was impossible. Brandon Lewis had Jolie with a knife to her throat. One stupid move on Mad Dog's part, and the boy could jerk his hand and slit her throat. If that wasn't bad enough, the man he suspected was Dwayne Duncan, aka Abdul Nadir, stood in front of the pair, holding a pistol pointed at Jolie's chest. Add the audience of jacked-up teens on motorcycles, and it was a powder keg with a lit fuse.

"Mad Dog, come in," a voice said into Mad Dog's ear.

"Mad Dog here," he whispered.

"Kujo here with Swede. You seeing what we're seeing?"

Mad Dog's released the breath he'd been holding. Some of the cavalry had arrived. Still, how was he going to get Brandon to drop his knife and Nadir his gun?

"I'm seeing it from the northeast corner of the house."

"Tree line on the other side of the motorcycle brigade from you," Kujo said. "Six with you?"

"He is."

"Be ready to send him in to stir things up. We can take the motorcyclists."

"The Lewis kid has a knife to Jolie's throat."

"She's CIA," Kujo reminded him. "She'll know what to do when Six makes his entrance. Kujo knows to go for the man with the gun."

"How do you know?"

Kujo chuckled. "I trained him." He gave Mad Dog the command. "Use it. Nadir won't know he's coming until he hits him."

"What if he gets a shot off before Six gets to him?"

"Swede here. Do you have another plan?" Swede jumped into the radio conversation. "Nadir is there to kill Agent Richards, one way or another. Don't waste another second. Her life depends on it."

"Roger." Mad Dog gave Six the command and watched as the German Shepherd stole through the night like a shadowy wolf stalking his prey. As he neared Nadir, he moved faster until he shot like a rocket and leaped from the side at Nadir's hand holding the gun.

A shot was fired.

Mad Dog didn't think about where the bullet went, he ran for Jolie.

She grabbed the hand holding the knife, bent Brandon's thumb back and twisted his arm under and behind his back.

Nadir kicked Six off his arm and aimed his pistol at Jolie.

Mad Dog dove in front of her, while aiming his nine-millimeter at Nadir. He pulled the trigger at the same time as Nadir's gun went off.

A sharp pain ripped through his side as he hit the ground, rolled to his feet and came up in a kneeling position, ready to fire again.

The pistol fell from Nadir's fingers. He clutched a hand to his chest and sank to the ground where he lay still.

The guys on the bikes revved their engines, but too late.

Swede and Kujo came at them from one end of the lineup, firing their handguns in the air and yelling like banshees.

The bikers spun out, racing for the road leading off the ranch.

"You need help?" Mad Dog yelled to Jolie.

"I've got this," Jolie answered, holding Brandon's arm high up the middle of his back. The teen danced on his toes, his face creased in pain.

Mad Dog gave Six the command to stay with Jolie,

and he followed Swede and Kujo, chasing after the bikers as they made their getaway.

As the riders reached the road, one by one, they were jerked off their bikes, landing hard on their backsides as if a giant hand knocked them off.

Ahead of him, Mad Dog saw Hank step out of the trees along with three other men. Swede, Kujo and Mad Dog converged on the bikers, tackled them and held them down.

Sirens blared and flashing lights blinked through the trees as county sheriff vehicles arrived, followed by a fire truck and an ambulance.

Mad Dog had pinned his biker face-down on the ground when Deputy Wells appeared at his side. "Don't worry about me," he bit out. "Jolie has one around the side of the house."

The deputy took off running. A few moments later, another deputy arrived to relieve Mad Dog of his gang member.

As soon as he was free, Mad Dog hurried toward the house. He hadn't gone far when Deputy Wells rounded the corner, leading Brandon Lewis in handcuffs. Jolie and Six walked alongside him.

Mad Dog ran toward Jolie.

When she saw him, she rushed forward and met him halfway, flinging her arms around his neck.

He swung her off her feed and around. "Thank God. Thank God," he said over and over. "I didn't know what had happened to you." He set her on her feet and scanned her body from head to toe. "Are you all right? Did he hurt you?" He paid particular attention to her throat where Brandon had held his knife to her perfect skin. "I died a thousand deaths watching him with that knife."

"He wasn't going to do it. Brandon wasn't going to kill me." Jolie shook her head. "His mother, Sherry, was going to, but Nadir killed her."

"That was Brandon's mother on the ground?" Mad Dog asked.

Jolie pinched the bridge of her nose. "What a mess. Remind me to tell you about it when we can catch our breath. The point is, you came at exactly the right moment. If you hadn't sent Six in when you did, Nadir would have shot me."

"I have Kujo to thank for that. He trained him to go after the guy with the gun." Mad Dog pulled her to him again and held her long and hard. "I almost lost you. I just found you, and I almost lost you."

She laughed, her voice catching on a sob. "All I could think about was what was happening to you. I didn't know if the house was burning down with you inside." Jolie pulled away just enough to look at her family home. "You put the fire out?"

Mad Dog nodded. "The extinguisher worked enough to douse the flame. Your house survived." And thankfully so had Jolie. His heart was full to the point it was painful. Now that it was all over, he felt weak with relief.

JOLIE HUGGED him around the middle, tears wetting his

shirt. She didn't know why, but Mad Dog made her feel things no other man made her feel.

"Hey, why are you crying? Everything turned out all right." He tipped up her chin and stared down into her face.

She stared up at him, his handsome face lit by the head-lights from the emergency vehicles parked in the yard.

"I was afraid I'd lose you," she admitted. "I didn't give a damn about the house. I was afraid I'd lose you."

Hank, Swede, Kujo, Bear and two other men surrounded Mad Dog, Jolie and Six.

Hank introduced the men they hadn't met as Viper and Boomer.

Swede hugged Jolie all the while shaking his head. "When I saw that kid with a knife to your neck, I thought for sure you were a goner. Glad you're still with the living. My fiancée, Allie, wouldn't forgive me if she didn't get to meet you."

"Thanks for coming to our rescue," she said. "I'd love to meet your fiancée." And she meant it. Already, she felt like she was one of Hank's team and belonged with this group of men and their women.

Swede glanced down at her shirt, his eyes narrowing. "Damn, girl, you're bleeding."

Jolie looked down at her side and her arm, surprised by the amount of blood. She patted her side but felt no pain. "I wasn't hit."

Her gaze shot to Mad Dog. His dark jacket glistened like it was wet. She reached out and touched it, her fingers coming away warm and wet. "You were hit!"

Mad Dog opened his jacket, the movement making him wince. "Damn. I think you're right. I guess I didn't notice in all the confusion."

"How could you not notice?" Jolie shook her head and yelled, "Medic!"

An EMT showed up. Hank and Swede helped Mad Dog onto a stretcher. The EMTs packed the wound to stem the flow of blood and hooked him up to an IV. Then they wheeled him away to the waiting ambulance.

Jolie hurried alongside him, holding his hand all the way. When they loaded him into the ambulance, she insisted on riding with him.

"Only family members are allowed," the EMT said.

"I'm his fiancée," she said.

The EMT grinned. "Then hop on in."

She rode with Mad Dog to the hospital in Bozeman. He held her hand for the entire hour it took to get there, reassuring Jolie he would be okay.

By the time the doctor and nurses cleaned the wound and stitched him up, it was past midnight, but Jolie didn't care. She didn't want to leave him for a minute, afraid that, if she did, something would happen, and she might never see him again.

She knew it was irrational, but she couldn't help it. Having had no family since losing her father, she didn't want to risk losing the one man who'd made her love life again.

If being with him meant giving up her career with the CIA, she'd do it happily. Besides, the Rocking R Ranch needed someone there who cared. Someone to call it home.

EPILOGUE

"JOLIE! THEY'RE HERE!" Mad Dog called out.

"Good. The lasagna is just about ready. Did you ice the beer?"

"I did. And a couple six packs of wine coolers and hard lemonade for those who don't like beer."

Jolie slipped an arm around his waist and stood with him on the newly repaired front porch. All signs of the burns and scorch marks had been replaced, sanded or painted. The exterior of her home had a fresh coat of paint and looked great.

Mad Dog's chest swelled with pride. He was glad he'd had the time to help with the repairs. He hadn't let a few stitches keep him from fully engaging in the repairs, even though Jolie had been on him every step of the way to take it easy.

The few weeks he'd been in Montana had been the happiest of his life. The more he got to know Jolie, the more he realized she was the woman for him. And, if he wasn't mistaken, she was pretty stuck on him, too. Which gave him the confidence to make the purchase he'd made the last time he'd visited Bozeman for his follow-up doctor's appointment when they'd removed his stitches.

He stuck his hand in his pocket, felt around for the ring and nearly had a heart attack when he didn't find it.

Jolie must have felt him flinch. "The scar still sore from them taking the stitches out?" she asked.

"Yeah. A little," he said. They were, but not enough to bother him. He slipped his hand into his other pocket and breathed a sigh of relief. The diamond engagement ring was there.

Trucks and SUVs pulled up to the house, and members of the Brotherhood Protectors team climbed out and helped their women alight.

Hank was first to the porch with Sadie and Emma. "The place looks great. I'm sure your father would be happy that you decided to keep it and reestablish the ranch."

Sadie hugged Jolie and handed Emma to Mad Dog. "Our housewarming gift will be delivered in a few days. I hope you don't mind that we didn't bring it with us." Her eyes danced with delight. "Tell them what it is, Hank. Tell them."

Hank laughed. "We got you a heifer. A registered Angus heifer."

Mad Dog laughed and shook Hank's hand.

Jolie clapped a hand over her mouth, tears springing to her eyes.

"It'll be the start of your herd," Mad Dog said, hugging her to his side.

Swede was next with a pretty, auburn-haired woman who bore a slight resemblance to Hank. "Sorry we haven't been by sooner, but we had to bring cattle in from the hills with the weather getting cooler," Swede said. "This is Allie, Hank's little sister and my fiancée. We're getting married next month and want you two to come to the wedding."

"We'd love to," Jolie replied and glanced over her shoulder at Mad Dog. "That is, if you aren't working."

"I'll have to check with my new boss." Mad Dog winked at Hank.

"I'm glad you decided to come to work for the Brotherhood Protectors," Hank said. "Word is spreading, and I have more work than men to fill the positions."

Mad Dog'd had a long talk with Greg Lambert about his work with the Sleeper SEALs and had agreed to be on call for future missions. In the meantime, he'd work as part of the Brotherhood Protectors with Hank. With so many ranchers selling their places to rich folk from the cities, the need for protection had grown in Montana. He'd be home when he could and help out on the ranch.

"I understand you left the CIA to ranch fulltime," Allie said. "I'm glad I'm not the only female rancher in the area. We'll have a lot to talk about."

Jolie agreed and made a date to have coffee with Allie soon.

Bear introduced her to his woman, Mia Chastain, a

Hollywood screenwriter Jolie knew from back in high school.

Mad Dog was amazed at how many people Jolie knew from growing up in Eagle Rock. He was glad she'd be surrounded by them. It made going away for his work easier, knowing she'd have people there to take care of her when she needed help.

Duke Morris and Angel Carson, both former Army Special Forces, were next to greet them. Followed by Taz Davil and Hannah Kendricks. Taz had been an Army Ranger, and Hannah worked with disabled vets and horses at the Brighter Days Rehab Ranch.

Kujo and his fiancée, Molly, arrived with Six and took up a couple of seats on the porch.

Boomer and his wife, Daphne, arrived with their baby Maya, followed by Viper, retired Delta Force, who'd hired on when Kujo came to work with Hank's team.

Once everyone was settled with drinks and snacks, Mad Dog couldn't wait another second.

He cleared his throat and asked everyone to come out on the porch, because he had an announcement to make.

Jolie joined him, frowning. "What announcement?"

"This one." He took her hand in his. "Jolie Richards, you are one of the smartest, bravest and most beautiful women I've ever met."

Her cheeks blossomed with color, and she looked around at the others all staring at her. "Thank you, Caleb, but shouldn't we feed our guests?"

"We will. When I'm finished." He hurried on before

he lost his nerve. Mad Dog drew in a deep breath and continued. "I never thought I was cut out for a family or relationships because of my not so wonderful upbringing, but it took knowing you to open my eyes to the possibilities. I realized I didn't have to follow in my father's footsteps. I never have and never will."

"You're a much better man," Jolie said. "My father would have loved you."

"I'm more concerned that you love me," he said and dropped to one knee.

Jolie's eyes filled with tears. "You aren't...you're not...oh, please, get up."

He laughed and shook his head. "I'm not finished.

Jolie dropped to her knees and held his hand in both of hers. "Go on," she whispered.

"Jolie Richards, I can't promise I'll always do the right thing or say the right thing, but I will promise to love you until the day I die, and probably even longer. What I'm trying to say is, will you marry me?"

"The ring," Sadie whispered. "Where's the ring?"

Mad Dog could have kicked himself. He fumbled in his pocket and pulled out the ring. "Well, will ya? If you say yes, you'll make me the happiest man alive. I swear I love you more than you can ever imagine."

She pressed a finger to his lips. "Shut up. Just shut up." And she kissed him.

He kissed her back, but then set her away from him. "Let me be perfectly clear. Is that a yes?"

She flung her arms around his neck, and they both fell over. "Yes!"

Mad Dog didn't care that they were lying on the

porch, and all of their guests were laughing. The woman he'd been looking for all of his life had just agreed to marry him. Life couldn't get any better than it was at that moment.

*

Find out who the Commander calls next. Make sure to pick up ALL the books in the Sleeper SEAL series. These can be read in any order and each stands alone.

x Protecting Dakota by Susan Stoker
Slow Ride by Becky McGraw
X Michael's Mercy by Dale Mayer
X Saving Zola by Becca Jameson
Bachelor SEAL by Sharon Hamilton
X Montana Rescue by Elle James
X Thin Ice by Maryann Jordan
Grinch Reaper by Donna Michaels
All In by Lori Ryan
Broken SEAL by Geri Foster
Freedom Code by Elaine Levine
X Flat Line by J.M. Madden

JOIN my Newsletter and find out about sales, free books, contests and new releases first!
https://ellejames.com/contact/

If you want to know when my books go on sale? Follow me on Bookbub!
https://www.bookbub.com/authors/elle-james

ALSO BY ELLE JAMES

SEAL's Seduction (#6)

SEAL'S Defiance (#7)

SEAL's Deception (#8)

SEAL's Deliverance (#9)

Ballistic Cowboy

Hot Combat (#1)

Hot Target (#2)

Hot Zone (#3)

Hot Velocity (#4)

Texas Billionaire Club

Tarzan & Janine (#1)

Something To Talk About (#2)

Who's Your Daddy (#3)

Love & War (#4)

Hellfire Series

Hellfire, Texas (#1)

Justice Burning (#2)

Smoldering Desire (#3) TBD

Up in Flames (#4) TBD

Plays with Fire (#5) TBD

Hellfire in High Heels (#6) TBD

Cajun Magic Mystery Series

Voodoo on the Bayou (#1)

Voodoo for Two (#2)

Deja Voodoo (#3)

Cajun Magic Mysteries Books 1-3

Billionaire Online Dating Service

The Billionaire Husband Test (#1)

The Billionaire Cinderella Test (#2)

The Billionaire Bride Test (#3) TBD

The Billionaire Matchmaker Test (#4) TBD

SEAL Of My Own

Navy SEAL Survival

Navy SEAL Captive

Navy SEAL To Die For

Navy SEAL Six Pack

Devil's Shroud Series

Deadly Reckoning (#1)

Deadly Engagement (#2)

Deadly Liaisons (#3)

Deadly Allure (#4)

Deadly Obsession (#5)

Deadly Fall (#6)

Covert Cowboys Inc Series

Triggered (#1)

Taking Aim (#2)

Bodyguard Under Fire (#3)

Cowboy Resurrected (#4)

Navy SEAL Justice (#5)

Navy SEAL Newlywed (#6)

High Country Hideout (#7)

Clandestine Christmas (#8)

Thunder Horse Series

High Octane Heroes

Haunted

Engaged with the Boss

Cowboy Brigade

Time Raiders: The Whisper

Bundle of Trouble

Killer Body

Operation XOXO

An Unexpected Clue

Baby Bling

Under Suspicion, With Child

Texas-Size Secrets

Cowboy Sanctuary

Lakota Baby

Dakota Meltdown

Beneath the Texas Moon

CPSIA information can be obtained
at www.ICGtesting.com
Printed in the USA
LVHW052006121218
600215LV00018B/660/P